In Those First Bright Days of Elvis

First Edition
Printed and Bound in the USA

ISBN: 978-1-942428-92-3

Cover painting by Josephine Rascoe Keenan
Cover design by Kimberly Pennell
Interior design by Kelsey Rice

~ THE DAYS OF ELVIS SERIES, BOOK I ~

In Those First Bright Days of Elvis

-BY-

JOSEPHINE RASCOE KEENAN

P
Pen-L Publishing
Fayetteville, Arkansas
Pen-L.com

Acknowledgements

I owe a debt of gratitude to my English teachers who impressed upon me the importance of clarity and accurate communication.

Many people helped me take this story from its bare-bones beginnings, which can be stated simply as "I want to tell people how wonderful it all was when Elvis first came on the scene and how his music enriched our lives" to "I need a plot and characters to do that."

Thanks to:

Duke and Kimberly Pennell, who thought my work was worthy of presenting to the world.

Sarah Hersh Dowlin, who believed in me and encouraged me before I had written a word on the page.

My colleagues in the writers group, whose suggestions and enthusiasm helped to guide my journey.

My husband, Frank, who patiently listened to me read the chapters aloud, over and over, through all the revisions, and offered so many insightful suggestions that steered me to the finished product; who took me to visit Graceland, the Rock and Roll Hall of Fame and Museum, and to numerous writers conventions where I learned valuable lessons and made many wonderful friends; and who, with his never-failing love and support, kept me on track through all the rejections as I struggled to catch the golden ring.

Dedicated to the memory of my mother,
Josephine Lawton Rascoe,
who sacrificed to provide me with an education
so that I could fulfill my dreams;
and to the memory of Elvis Aaron Presley,
whose music filled our lives with joy.

Contents

CHAPTER 1
The Hillbilly Amateur Show

From my seat behind the stage in the Market Square Arena in Indianapolis, all I could see of the star performer was his gyrating backside. Glaring spotlights revealed the outline of his underpants through his white suit.

While he sang the final song, an assistant hung scarves around his neck, which he passed on to screaming audience members. Every aspect of his person radiated exhaustion. He was about to give away the last scarf when he glanced over his shoulder and saw me. He cocked his head, his face quizzical. I moved to the edge of the stage. A woman snatched at the scarf, but he reached past her and draped it around my neck, his eyes still questioning.

Knowing he'd never hear me, even if I yelled in his ear, I gestured to myself and, with exaggerated lips, mouthed, "Juliet."

A smile touched his face. He had time only to nod before applause and screams forced him back into the world of fame, where his ambition and his unforgettable voice had imprisoned him.

I tried to go backstage after the show, but his guards were not convinced I was a friend. Less than two months later, he was dead. This was the end of the story—the last, sad days of his life. But I saw him perform in a little town in Arkansas during his first, bright days.

The occasion was The Free Hillbilly Amateur Show. His star was low on the horizon at that time, but it would soon blaze like a supernova in the sky.

The sun had long set, but the air still burned hot as a by-product at eight o'clock that October night when we four rushed up to the gates of Memorial Stadium. At the back of the crowd, waiting to get in, I pointed to the poster of the show's feature attraction.

"Who is this Elvis guy, anyway?"

"They say he's on his way to the top," Della said.

"And playing in El Dorado, Arkansas?" I tapped my foot. "I never heard of him."

Faye shrugged. "Oh well. When have we ever turned down a free show?"

Della peered into Rhonda's face. "You're getting another pimple. You need to use that cream I told you about."

Rhonda stuck out her tongue.

I straightened Della's Peter Pan collar. "Your new pink blouse is the most. A birthday present?"

"Yes, but my big present is Daddy letting me have the car tonight for the first time."

Without thinking, I blurted out, "Mama made me wait till I turned fifteen, too."

The girls gave me their familiar, pitying looks that said they knew I had no dad. I pressed my fingers against the shame that flared up in my cheeks whenever my gimped family came into focus. In truth, I did have one, but no sane person would call him a dad.

Rhonda pulled a compact out of her purse and checked first one area then another of her face in the small mirror.

"Maylene McCord's been getting the car since she turned fourteen."

I sighed. "Maybe that's why she's radioactive popular. Look at her, up there in front with her in-crowd cronies."

Della frowned. "She could put someone's eye out, swinging that foot-long ponytail around."

"She calls it her 'crown in glory,'" Rhonda said, tossing her head as if she could swing instead of wag her two-inch ponytail. "You know, like the hymn."

"Think they'll save us seats?" I asked with a cynical laugh.

"They act like we've got cooties!" Faye jerked up her chin. "Who wants to sit with them, anyway?"

Della tapped Faye's nose with a finger. "You do, for one."

"Let's face it," I said. "We all do."

Della snorted. "They don't hobnob with Dilberts, as they so charmingly refer to us."

My sphere of influence consisted of these three friends. I'd do better to call it my sphere of *no* influence, for we fabulous four—joke—could not influence the in-crowd to acknowledge our existence. I guess if I were one of them, I'd feel the same way about us groveling Dilberts—so anxious to please, always hoping that today they'd speak to us in the halls, choose us for their team, invite us to go to the Dairyette with them. We tried so hard, but to the mighty in-crowd, we remained invisible. "Try, try, cry, cry."

To be totally honest, all our efforts shimmered with rage about the way they treated us, so who could blame them? *At least we four have each other. Or so I thought.*

A tall, lanky guy with dishwater-blond hair squeezed his way through the crowd to Maylene's group. I shifted my stance to get a better view of him.

"Hubba hubba! Who's that?"

"I've seen him around," Rhonda said. "He's older. First year college, I think."

I fanned myself with my hand. "Wow! He's so cute! Does somebody in that crowd go with him?"

Della shrugged. "Who knows, and who cares?"

I gave her a sly grin. "I do, for one."

The gates swung open, and we inched inside and up the bleacher steps. I canvassed the seating area.

"Maylene's group is over there in the center section."

Della squinted. "Well, they're not beckoning to us. I can see that much without my glasses."

The bleachers, still hot from the southern sun beating down on them all day, heated our fannies as we settled a few rows behind them. A makeshift, wooden platform on the stadium grass served as a stage. Five contestants in the preshow talent competition bleated their songs to an inattentive crowd.

My gaze drifted over the bleachers, and adrenalin flushed through me. Off to the right, about ten rows down, sat my father. Even from that far away, I could tell he was unshaven. I hadn't seen him in five months, and I didn't want to see him for another five, if ever. But hard as I tried, I couldn't keep my eyes off him.

Removing a small flask from his pocket, he stole a glance over his shoulder. I dodged behind the blue-haired lady in front of me, but not before seeing him take a quick nip.

"Will you change seats with me, Della?" I asked, churning to get out of his line of vision.

"What for?"

"I just want to sit on the aisle."

She groaned and picked up her purse. "I guess so."

The audience jeered as the off-key talent show winner clutched his prize of a seventy-five dollar bond and clomped off the stage. Three musicians clattered on behind him, lugging music stands and chairs.

"That's the backup group for the feature attraction," Della said.

The three warmed up their instruments with a din of discordant noise. People stomped their feet on the bleachers until finally the MC, dressed in a candy-striped, red-and-white jacket, leaped upon the platform.

"Ladies and Gentlemen, thank you for your patience."

The crowd guffawed.

"You're going to love our show!" he shouted into the mic. "At this time, I am happy to introduce the boys accompanying tonight's feature attraction. Please hold your applause until the last."

The crowd hooted.

The MC shouted again. "Please welcome Scotty Moore on guitar, Bill Black on upright bass, and D. J. Fontana on drums!"

People made sloppy slaps.

"And now, ladies and gentlemen, that rockabilly, bopping hillbilly," he paused for effect, "Mr. Elll—vis Presley!"

With a sheepish smile, the new singer ran out from underneath the bleachers, carrying his guitar. His dark hair was combed back off his forehead in pompadour style. He wore violet pants, a black shirt, an orange jacket, and white bucks.

I bounced on the bleacher. "Get a load of that outfit."

Della sneered. "He looks like a hood with the sideburns and ducktail."

"No boy I know would be caught dead dressed like that," said Rhonda.

I laughed. "Your precious Eugene Hoffmeyer's been wearing mismatched clothes since seventh grade."

"That doesn't make him a hood."

"I didn't say it did."

"You *insinuated* it did. I don't like it when people insinuate stuff. Just last week, Maylene McCord insinuated I was stupid."

"What did she say?"

"She said, 'Rhonda, you're stupid.'"

We cracked up.

Elvis Presley's penetrating eyes swept the audience. He strummed a chord.

"Folks, I'm gonna start with 'That's All Right.'"

"Hurry up, or you'll be ending with that, too!" a man yelled.

Elvis signaled his musicians, and they launched into the music—wild and loud. He gyrated, twisted his hips, and squatted low. Suddenly, he jerked his face from profile to front and fixed the audience with a powerful stare.

I leaped up, screaming.

"Julie Morgan!" Della yanked at me. "What's the matter with you?"

I dropped into a squat, arms covering my head, in case my father was looking, along with everyone else.

"I couldn't help it!" I yelled over the blaring music. I eased back onto the bleacher. "Dig that sound! That's not country. It's different."

The singer rolled up and down on the balls of his feet, his hair flopping over his eyes. Grabbing the slender pole that held the mic, he slung it back and forth, rolling its base in a circle.

"I heard he dates a girl here in town," Rhonda said.

"You don't mean?" I said.

"It's rumored he gave her a pink Cadillac! We drove by her house one night last week."

Della crossed her eyes to signal Rhonda, but she didn't notice. "Her front door was open, and she was standing just inside with a light shining behind her."

I felt like she'd slapped me in the face. "We, who, drove by her house?"

"We all—oops." Rhonda tucked her chin.

"Rhonda, you weren't supposed to tell." Della dropped her head into her hands.

I grabbed Rhonda's arm. "You got the car for the first time . . . and you didn't come by for me?"

"I only got it for an hour and on the spur of the moment. We didn't have time to go all the way over to your house."

"You can go from one end of this town to the other in five minutes," I said.

A barrier of raucous music fell between us. I stared at the stage with unseeing eyes, wondering what else they had left me out of.

The end of the number met with rousing applause. Immediately, Elvis launched into another. For a while, we watched the show, saying nothing. Then Rhonda turned to me.

"We didn't mean to leave you out. We just wanted to get a load of the car and cast an eyeball at a girl who's done IT."

"What makes you think she's done IT?"

"By the way she stood, slouched, with her pelvis slung out."

"That's stupid," I said. "You slouch. Have you been doing IT?"

She put on a pious face. "Nice girls don't do IT until they're married."

I raised one eyebrow. "A nice girl might for a pink Cadillac."

The song ended abruptly. In the silent split second before the applause, Rhonda's voice rang out, "For a guy to give you a car, you'd have to do IT!" And everybody around us heard.

She clapped her hand over her mouth, and we leaned away from her, hiding our faces.

When everyone had turned back around from gawking, I said, "Did you see the car?"

Rhonda said, "No. But she's no virgin. I'd bet my life on that."

Elvis lunged to the floor again.

"His music drives me out of my tree," I said.

At intermission, I spent the last of my allowance at the concession stand for a coke in a sweaty paper cup and gave it to Della.

"Happy birthday."

At that moment, the college boy passed near me. Our eyes met for a second, then he moved on through the stragglers heading back to their seats.

We had returned to our bleacher when a girl I had never seen before came up the steps of the grandstand. She looked about our age. Like me, she wore a black skirt and a pink peasant blouse, but her skirt wrinkled around her thighs, and her blouse was pulled off the shoulders so low you could see her cleavage. She didn't seem to notice us, but my heart jumped as she got closer.

Faye clutched my arm. "My God, Julie, that girl is the spitting image of you!"

CHAPTER 2
SEEING DOUBLE

Della, Rhonda, and Faye looked again and again, from me to my lookalike, who sat back a ways across the aisle with a woman wearing a low-cut dress and tarnished earrings that dangled to her shoulders.

"Will you all stop that?" I said.

Rhonda giggled. "I feel like I'm seeing double."

"Don't be stupid. We don't look *that* much alike," I said.

"You look exactly alike," Della stated flatly.

Faye elbowed Rhonda. "Here comes your boyfriend."

Eugene Hoffmeyer, Dilbert of all Dilberts, clomped up the bleacher steps toward us. The blue elephant pattern on his pink shirt labeled him totally square.

The only claim Rhonda had on him was that, because they lived on the same street, their parents had taken turns driving them to the dances last year in ninth grade. Lately, he'd been bugging me to go on a "coke date" with him. Although I had never accepted, if Rhonda found out he'd asked, she'd have a cow.

"Hey, girls," he said, plopping down next to me, "when you gonna slip me some lip?"

His breath smelled of hot dog, and a smidgen of mustard lingered on the side of his mouth.

Della made the throw-up sign—a finger down her throat.

"Glad you could make the scene," he said. "I see you still haven't weaseled your way into the in-crowd."

Rhonda leaned around me. "Eugene, I hear you're getting the car these days."

He puffed out his chest. "Right on!"

I stared at him with wide eyes, warning him through mental telepathy not to let on that he'd asked me out.

Rhonda batted her eyelashes. "Mom's finally said I can go on dates."

"Uh oh," he muttered, looking toward the grandstand show where Elvis still sang and gyrated under the stadium lights.

"Sooo," Rhonda said, tucking her chin and looking at him from beneath lowered lashes, "you could take me to the Dairyette tonight after the show."

"Aw, I can't," Eugene said and gave me a conspiratorial look that no one could miss.

Rhonda's face collapsed. "I can't believe this!" she said. Leaping up, she barreled down the steps and out of the grandstand.

Della narrowed her eyes at Eugene. "I saw that look you gave Julie."

Faye glared. "Have you two been sneaking around behind Rhonda's back?"

I rolled my eyes. "You both know better than that! Besides, how could we sneak? Everyone in this town knows what you're going to do before you know yourself."

"You didn't know Rhonda got her car until she told you!" Della said. *Rub it in!*

"Now, Julie," Eugene said, his eyes glinting mischief, "go ahead. Tell them you went on a coke date with me."

"Eugene Hoffmeyer! I have never set foot in your car!"

Della shook her finger at me. "Well, I'll be diddly-dog damned. I thought you were Rhonda's friend. If you'd do this to her, you'd do it to all of us."

"I've never had a date at all! With *any* boy!"

"Don't try to play innocent. I'm on to you, Julie Morgan." She jumped up. "I guess we don't need to worry about how you'll get home! Come on, Faye. Let's catch up with Rhonda."

With scathing looks at Eugene and me, they stomped off.

I turned on him. "Why on earth would you say we had a coke date? Now they're furious with me! I may not have a ride."

"I'll take you home."

"No way!"

I tore down the stadium steps. By the time I got to the gates, the girls were nowhere in sight. I darted across the asphalt parking lot to where we'd left the car. The space was empty. My heart beat faster. Maybe I was in the wrong place. I rushed around looking, but the car was gone.

Now what? If I called Mama to come get me, she'd never let me go with Della and them again. Back inside the gates, I watched people straggle up to the concession stand. After a few minutes, a big finale resounded from inside the stadium, followed by pounding applause, and people began streaming out.

Intent on chatting with her group, Maylene McCord bumped into me as they hurried past.

"Excuse me," she said, barely glancing up.

I opened my mouth to ask her for a ride but then closed it, unable to bear hearing the flimsy excuse she'd give me. I watched until she and her flock, with their happy chatter and bright smiles, melted into the glowing night. Elvis Presley, now wearing all black, came out to sign autographs. I searched for anyone I knew among the collage of faces surrounding him.

Too drunk to notice me, my father passed so close I could smell whiskey fumes reeking from him. Heading through the gate into the parking lot, he stumbled and pitched toward the asphalt. Someone caught him by the elbow. Once steadied, he moved on into the night.

I boiled inside. Not that I would dare get into the car with him when he was drunk, but what kind of man was he that couldn't be relied on to give his own daughter a ride home when she was alone and stranded? No wonder folks around town treated Mama and me like we were second-class citizens.

In the press of the throng, my mysterious lookalike also passed, so close I could smell her sachet—Chantilly—the same kind I wore. The tarnished-earrings woman walked slightly ahead of her, smoking. Mama always said ladies never walked with a cigarette in their hand.

As they crept along in the crowd, moving toward the parking lot, my lookalike happened to glance in my direction. Stunned shock registered on her face. She stopped still. From a few steps ahead, the woman looked back at her.

"Carmen! Come on!"

"But—"

The woman saw me and drew a quick breath. "Come on, Carmen," she said, giving the girl a nudge.

All the way across the parking lot, the girl kept looking back at me. I watched until they were lost in the glitz of shiny cars.

Eventually, Elvis disappeared somewhere back inside the stadium. Still, I sifted through the thinning crowd for anyone I knew. Rowdy kids revved their engines and shot off into the night. Old folks glided away in their sleek, chromed chariots. The place was almost deserted.

By now, I had chewed a fingernail down to the quick. It was at least three miles to my house, and the streetlights were out in some areas along the way. I shouldn't have been so quick to blow off Eugene.

"You look like you might be lost," said a voice at my shoulder.

Startled, I turned. The ice-blue eyes of Elvis Presley gazed into mine. I couldn't utter an intelligent word.

"Uh, maybe, I mean no…well, yes, sort of!"

He smiled. "Did you like the show?"

For a moment, I just stood there, nodding. Then it dawned on me. He wanted a compliment.

"Your music is really different," I blurted.

His eyes danced. "You think so?"

"Oh, yes. *Very* different!"

A grin took over his whole face. He did a huge gyration, right there at the gates of the stadium.

"So, what are you doing out here all by yourself?"

I hesitated. "My friends left me, and I don't have a way home."

He cocked his head and smiled sideways. "Well, tell me something. Have you ever ridden in a pink Cadillac?"

CHAPTER 3
THE PINK CADILLAC

Walking across the deserted parking lot with Elvis, I searched for something to say.

"You seem all rattled," he said.

"I saw a stranger tonight who looks enough like me to be my twin."

"Whoa, that would shake you up! Who do you reckon she is?"

"I don't have a clue."

We were quiet for a few seconds before he said, "I had a twin, a real one. He was born dead."

"Oh, that's so sad."

"You got that right. I don't think my mama'll ever get over it. And me, I've always felt lonely, even incomplete somehow—like half of my soul is missing."

He looked me straight in the eyes. "You're an understanding kind of girl, you know that?"

His Cadillac was pink-frosting scrumptious. He opened the door for me, and I had one foot inside when the sensible voice in my head echoed one of Mama's refrains, "Don't get into cars with strangers."

I pulled back. "On second thought, you probably don't have time to take me home."

"Got plenty. We don't leave for Cleveland until tomorrow." He steered me into the car and shut the door.

As he jogged around to the driver's side, sensible advised, "Break and run." But my romantic voice said, "Take a chance."

"All I have to do tonight is party!" he said, slipping behind the wheel and turning the ignition key.

As I tried to sneak a glance at my watch, he pointed to the dashboard with a knowing smile.

"There's a clock right there. What time do you have to be home?"

"Not a second after eleven."

"No sweat. It's barely ten thirty."

We peeled out and headed north. "This car's all souped-up," he said. "Get ready for a thrill."

I frantically gestured toward the rear window. "My house is the opposite way."

"I thought we'd stop off at Old Hickory first. Are you hungry? I'm starved and so dry I could spit cotton. Don't worry, honey. My mama raised me right. I'll get you home safe."

His smile made me feel better.

"Why don't you put your window down?" he said.

I reached for the crank to roll it down, but there wasn't one.

Elvis laughed. "Press the button on the armrest."

"Wow! The girls would go ape if they got a load of this!"

The air rushing in through the open windows blew my hair sky west and crooked as we sped down the highway, past the Dairyette toward Old Hickory.

"This car gives me a charge!" I said. "The dashboard lights look like the inside of a space ship! Is it an Eldorado?"

"It's a Fleetwood. I bought it when my first Cadillac caught fire and burned up."

"I love the color."

"It was blue when I got it, but I had it painted with a color formula made 'specially for me called Elvis Rose."

"How can you afford to buy a Cadillac, playing at free amateur shows?"

"I've made a few bucks on my record, 'That's All Right.' Cut it a year ago. And all my shows are free. Hey, tell me something, honey. You pronounce the 'Eldorado' in the Cadillac right. How come folks around here can't pronounce the name of the town?"

"El-duh-ray-duh is right. It's just not the Spanish way."

He chuckled. "It's the hillbilly way, huh?"

He turned off the main highway into Old Hickory's parking lot and honked for curb service.

While we waited for the carhop to come out, I combed my tangled hair with my fingers and racked my brain for anything—even something dumb—to say.

A dark-blue Chrysler Imperial pulled up, and the college boy we had seen at the concert got out and sauntered across the parking lot. On the way, he noticed Elvis's car, and his face registered admiration. His eyes found me. A quizzical expression flashed across his face. Then, with a slight shrug, he headed inside.

"You're awful quiet," Elvis said.

I cleared my throat. "You seem to know El Dorado pretty well."

Twisting the rearview mirror so he could see himself, he spit on his palms and slicked back his hair.

"Yep, I hang around here a lot."

"Dating that girl you gave the pink Cadillac to?"

He jerked his chin toward me. "Where did you get that notion?"

"That's the word, humming bird."

He laughed. " If I did date a girl around here, I would never kiss and tell."

"What'll ya have?" the carhop asked at the car window.

"A coke and a pig sandwich," Elvis said. "Want one, honey?"

"Just a coke."

Inside the restaurant, somebody put money in the jukebox, and the outside speakers poured the latest pop hit into the night. Elvis dabbed at his pompadour and looked at me with brooding eyes.

"What's your name again?"

"I don't think I told you. It's Julie."

"That's nice. Is your real name Juliet?"

"No, just plain Julie."

"You're not *plain* anyone. You're beautiful."

My cheeks warmed.

"You look like I always imagined a Juliet would look. Mind if I call you that?"

A thrill scurried down my back.

"Juliet, I get a real kick out of giving gifts to people I like, and I like you. I want to give you a gift."

I swallowed hard. Maybe I didn't want a car after all.

"Would I have to . . . uh . . . do something for it?"

"Well, I do want something from you, Juliet."

My mind spun.

He leaned toward me.

I closed my eyes and turned my face up for my first kiss.

"Look at me, Juliet. Different good, or different bad?"

I blinked. "What?"

"You said my singing was different. I want to be a big star, the movies even. I need you to tell me—different good, or different bad?"

He was so nice, I wanted him to make it big, even though the truth was I didn't think he ever would. He searched my face intently, as if my answer would somehow have the power to determine his fate. I forced enthusiasm into my voice.

"Oh, different good! Definitely different good!"

"But how? In what way?" His tone was urgent.

I thought so hard my nose wrinkled. His dream seemed farfetched, except for one thing.

"You made me scream."

"Was that you?"

I tucked my head.

"But what made you scream?"

"I . . . I just couldn't help myself."

"Try to put your finger on what it was."

I thought hard.

"Your voice touches deep in my insides, somehow, and the way you wiggle and gyrate around makes me crazy."

"You know who I learned that from? Preachers."

I could feel my jaw go slack. "Preachers?"

He grinned. "We used to go to these religious singings all the time. Seemed like nobody reacted to the singers, but when the preachers started cuttin' up and jumpin' on the piano and movin' every which away, the audiences went nuts. I reckon I picked it up from them. You're the first, Juliet. Someday, I'll have 'em all screamin.'"

Roger Williams' "Autumn Leaves" blared out from the jukebox. Elvis threw open the car door, grabbed my hand, and pulled me across the seat.

"Let's dance."

I hesitated.

"Come on, Lady Juliet. Other couples are dancing beside their cars."

So I went with the moment. Elvis sang softly in my ear. Real autumn leaves from the elm tree beside the building drifted down around us in the bright lights of the parking lot.

"Are you a music lover, Juliet?"

"Yes. I play clarinet in the band. Someday, if I'm good enough, I want to play with a symphony orchestra."

"Have confidence, and you will. That's more important than talent or money. If you've got confidence, you can do anything."

Just as we got back in the car, the waitress came out and hooked our tray of food onto the lowered window on the driver's side.

"Do you know who I am, honey?" Elvis asked the carhop.

She frowned. "Should I?"

"Maybe not yet, but you will. Someday, when you see my name in lights, remember that on—what's the date?"

The carhop shrugged. "Uh, the seventeenth, I think."

"Mark it down," Elvis said. "On October seventeenth, 1955, you served Elvis Presley a pig sandwich right here in El Dorado, Arkansas. Oops! What time is it?"

"Oh my God," I said. "Seven minutes till."

"Eleven? Take the tray back," he told the carhop. "We gotta agitate the gravel!"

Gnawing his sandwich, he spun off. The harvest moon bobbed up on the horizon, and by the time he screeched to a stop in front of the house, it dangled like a giant, orange balloon above the old Sycamore tree.

"I'd take you to the bash for me and the boys," he said, turning off the engine, "if you weren't so young."

"Mama would never let me go. Thanks again for the ride. And good luck."

"I haven't hit the charts yet, but I will. I've got a feeling you're my good luck charm."

"Me? How could I be?"

"For starters, I never knew a girl named Juliet."

You still don't.

"But when you said my singing made you scream, it gave me that final ounce of confidence I need to make it all the way to the top."

I didn't think this greaser sitting across from me in a *pink* car with his strange, new music had a prayer. Then I remembered how my knees went weak when his deep, baritone voice rang out over the audience, and how his fast numbers made me crazy-wild, mad, insane.

"You know what, Elvis? You just *might* make it. I'll be rooting for you."

"I *will* make it, and when I'm in fat city, I won't forget you, Juliet."

He reached over into the backseat and fumbled around inside a cardboard box.

"Here's the present I want to give you." Taking a pen from the glove compartment, he scribbled on a glossy, black-and-white picture of himself. With a bashful grin, he held it out to me, along with a forty-five record of "That's All Right."

"Gee, thanks." I read, "'To Juliet, my good luck charm, with best wishes always, Elvis Presley.'"

"Now, remember what I said about having confidence."

That sounded like a cue for me to exit this unimaginable scene, but when I reached to open the door, I couldn't find the handle.

"I like to never've found it either, my first ride in a Cadillac," he said.

Leaping out, he ran around and opened the door for me, then gave me his arm as we went up the stone walkway to the front porch.

Mama had left the front door open, but as usual, the screen was latched, forcing me to bang so she'd know what time I got home. She was nowhere in sight. Elvis dodged the bugs dancing around the circular light fixture above us.

"Tell your daddy he needs to put up a yellow light bulb so the bugs'll leave you alone."

Familiar embarrassment crept over me. I bit back the impulse to say, "Oh sure, I'll call him right up. He's always so helpful."

Elvis put his hands on my waist and leaned toward me. Once again, I closed my eyes for my first kiss. I could feel his warm breath.

"Julia Lawrence Morgan!"

My eyes flew open. Mama stood, glaring, on the other side of the screen door.

"Evening, ma'am." Elvis backed a step away and tipped an imaginary hat. "Just delivering your daughter to the door."

"Do you know what time it is?" Mama arched one eyebrow, her standard method of showing disapproval.

I came to my senses. "Mama, this is Elvis Presley, the star of the show tonight at the stadium. The girls went off and left me, and Elvis was nice enough to bring me home."

Mama took in his hair and clothes. "You can't be a Southern boy."

"Yes'm, I am. Born and raised in Tupelo, Mississippi. I call Memphis home now." He bounced off the porch steps and backed a little ways down the walk. "Don't mean to be rude, but I gotta run. Remember what I told you, Juliet."

With a wink, he headed for his car.

"What's this 'Juliet' business? And what, pray, did he tell you?" Mama asked, unlatching the screen.

"Oh, just how a yellow light bulb could bring happiness to the Morgan household," I said.

She expelled an exasperated breath and locked the front door.

"He's going all the way to the top, Mama."

"From El Dorado, Arkansas?" Mama scoffed.

"And in a pink Cadillac!"

"A pink Cadillac?"

Mama's eyes grew big. She threw open the door and rushed out on the porch, craning her neck in both directions for a glimpse of Elvis's dazzling car. But he had already left on his journey.

My spirits sank when she came back inside and told me the news. "The second Great Depression called just before you got home."

"I saw him stumbling around at the concert. I wish he would leave me alone." I balled my fists. "I don't want to visit him, ever."

CHAPTER 4
That's All Right

Next morning, first thing, I put on the new forty-five record Elvis gave me. The music revived that wild feeling from the concert. Mama rushed in to my room from the kitchen.

"What is that music? It makes me want to scream."

"'That's All Right.'"

"No, it's not all right!"

"That's the name of it, and it's supposed to make you scream."

"I hope it doesn't rob you of your morals," she said.

"Is it robbing you of yours?" I laughed.

"That's enough of your sass, young lady. Hop, skip, and jump. You're going to be late to school. Salt mackerel for breakfast."

"Earp slop, bring the mop," I said, heading for the shower.

"Your hair looks pretty this morning," Mama said as I came into the breakfast room after my shower. "So fashionable with that wave falling close to one eye."

"Mama, I have to tell you something."

"Turn on the dope machine before you sit down, please."

"What channel?" I asked, heading into the den—formerly a long, skinny porch Mama had enclosed that stretched clear across the back of the house and our only room with air conditioning. Two red corduroy couches, each with two rectangular pillows for backs, sat opposite each other and lent a modern touch to the otherwise antique-filled bungalow. We could see the TV through the windows in the breakfast room.

She frowned. "It's so hard to decide now that we've got two. Channel eight has the best news. No, put on ten. No, eight."

I turned on the TV to channel eight, came back into the breakfast room, and slid into my chair.

"Aren't you glad I talked you into buying it?"

Mama gave me a fractured smile. "I never thought I would after that time at Mavis's, but now I don't know what I'd do without it, even if it does have me snoring at eight o'clock every night."

The husband of Mama's card-playing buddy, Mavis, owned a radio store. One Saturday morning, a bunch of friends had gathered in their living room around a huge wooden console with a small, circular screen about ten inches in diameter. At first, I'd thought it was a fancy radio.

"It's a television set," Mavis told us. "See the cowboy on his horse?"

We stared intently at the little screen.

"All I see is a maze of jiggling dots," Mama said.

"They must be having bad weather in Little Rock." Mavis adjusted the knobs. "In New York, you can see pictures on TV as plain as I see you right now. Look! There he is! See him?"

Not even a shadow was visible among the dots on the screen.

"You need to have your eyes examined," Mama said.

Mavis wagged a finger at Mama. "TV is the wave of the future."

"It's not the wave of *my* future," Mama had said in the car on the way home. "I'll never waste my hard-earned money buying a machine to watch jiggling snow."

"It could be the only way we'll ever see a white Christmas here in South Arkansas," I quipped. "After you buy the set, it's free."

"Till they think up some way to charge folks for thin air," Mama said.

But, a year later, they built a reception tower only eighty miles away in Monroe, and these days Mama often came home for lunch to watch her favorite soap.

"What was it you wanted to tell me?" Mama asked as I reached for the cream. "About the girls leaving you at the stadium? The very idea!"

"It's not that. Mama, I saw—."

"That Elvis fellow didn't try anything, did he?"

"He was all set to kiss me at the door, then you materialized."

Mama's left eyebrow shot up. "I hope you weren't on the verge of permitting a total stranger to take liberties."

"You mean it's all right for a boy who's *not* a total stranger to take liberties?" I asked, faking wide-eyed innocence.

"Julie Morgan!" She frowned and shook her head.

I reached for the cream.

"Speaking of your father." She forked up a bite of mackerel.

"Were we speaking of him?"

"I hear on the q.t. that he finally landed another job. Not likely he'll keep it. He's a scoundrel, now turned bum. In the five years I was married to him, he blew every dime my daddy left me. Now I have to work like a dog for peanuts."

"Listen, Mama, last night I saw a girl I've never seen before, at school or anywhere, and dig this—she's the spittin' image of me."

Mama got up and swished into the kitchen, calling back over her shoulder, "I don't know what your generation is coming to, using language like 'dig this.' It's bad enough you contemplated allowing that Elvis person to kiss you. For all you know, he's a common masher."

She'd keel over dead if she knew that I had contemplated a whole lot more than kissing.

"What's a masher?"

"You'll get the picture if you ever run across one. Did you notice what I dug out today?" she asked, coming back with the coffeepot. She twirled, and her pink skirt flared. "I'm *thinking pink*, so don't say I'm not hip."

"Mama, who could she be?"

"Who could who be?"

"The girl I saw last night."

She reached for the sugar dish. "Don't ask me. Probably some long-lost cousin. I need you to start supper when you get home from school today. Lawyer Baird is taking depositions, and I'll have to stay late to type them."

"Okay, but Mama, the woman she was with called her Carmen. Do you know anyone named Carmen?"

Mama pushed back her chair and headed into the kitchen. "Only that saucy, Latin movie star, Carmen Miranda. I was so sad when she passed away. You need to sashay."

"No, I mean someone around here!"

She looked at her watch. "Eight fifteen? I need to sashay myself."

When I followed her into the kitchen and took my plate to her at the sink, she said something so low I couldn't hear it over the sound of running water.

"What?" I said.

"The woman, what did she look like?"

"What woman?"

"The one with the girl named Carmen!"

"You don't have to yell, Mama. Long, dangling earrings. Walked with a cigarette in her hand. I don't know, just a woman. I want to talk about the girl, not the woman. Could I have a long-lost twin?"

"You have the most vivid imagination."

"I didn't imagine her. Della, Rhonda, and Faye saw her, too."

CHAPTER 5
Cast Away

From across the school grounds, I scanned the clusters of kids hanging around waiting for the bell, but my lookalike was not among them.

Della, Rhonda, and Faye were in our usual place on the steps by the flagpole. As I approached them, Faye kept her eyes trained on an open book, and Rhonda outright turned her back on me.

"Mom said I had to apologize for leaving you at the stadium last night, Julie," Della said, "but I'm not sorry. I see Eugene got you home all right."

A car horn blared in front of the school, announcing the arrival of the in-crowd carpool members. Maylene and her group piled out, their faces bright. Kids waved and instantly rushed over to lionize them.

"I get so tired of watching this show every day," Faye said. "You'd think President Eisenhower was driving up."

"Meanwhile, back at the ranch," Della said, "what are we going to do about Julie going out with Eugene?"

"I haven't gone out with him! I have zero interest in Eugene Hoffmeyer! And he didn't take me home last night."

Rhonda looked back at me from over her shoulder, a flicker of hope in her eyes. "He didn't?"

"No."

Her face sagged with relief.

"Too bad you had to walk," Faye said, "but if you ask me, it's what you deserved."

"I didn't have to walk."

Rhonda put a hand on her hip. "Then how did you get home?"

"You'll never believe this. Elvis Presley gave me a ride home!"

Rhonda looked puzzled. "Who?"

"The star of the show. And get this—in a pink Cadillac!"

Their faces registered total disbelief.

Faye broke the silence. "You're right, we'll never believe that."

"It's true. Ask my mother. She met him."

"Sure," Della scoffed. "And I'm gonna be homecoming queen. Why don't you just admit that Eugene took you home, instead of making up some lie about that singer?"

The first bell rang out.

"It's true!" I yelled as they flounced toward the building, leaving me behind. The wind blew my hair into my eyes as I lurched after them. "Wait! I can prove it. He gave me his picture."

They ignored me. On the way to homeroom, I realized I had on one brown shoe and one black one. It was going to be a bad day.

Without them, I had no one to talk to but Eugene. When he sat down with me at lunch, Rhonda rushed out of the cafeteria in tears. Faye and Della huffed after her.

The next day, I held up Elvis's picture, like a cross before a vampire, as I approached them at the flagpole.

"See, I wasn't lying."

Della gave it a cursory glance. "We're not stupid, Julie. They sold those pictures all through the show."

"I didn't *buy* this! If you recall, I spent my last dime on a coke for you."

They turned their backs on me.

Alone all day, I wandered zombie-like from class to class. At noon, Rhonda dragged Eugene to their table. She, Della, and Faye gloated at the sight of me sitting by myself. They walked by me in the hall, like I wasn't there.

Being as isolated as a polio carrier was not doing wonders for my self-esteem. I dropped everything I picked up. Even with matching shoes on, I stumbled around, bumping into people, like I had four feet. I wanted to shrink up and disappear. I was a nobody who had lost her nobody friends.

We girls often squabbled, and one would be cast out to suffer, friendless, until she begged to be forgiven for the perceived offense. After the apology, the other three would "search their souls" before reluctantly allowing the offender back into the group. I'd already been shut out once since school started the day after Labor Day. The shunning never lasted more than two days. Tomorrow would be the third day of my exile.

This time, I refused to apologize for something I hadn't done. Consequently, on Friday, the fourth miserable day, I remained an outcast.

Sunday evening after supper, as I struggled with my French homework at the table, Mama looked up from the sink.

"What's the matter, sweetie? You're not yourself, and the phone hasn't rung for a week."

I sighed and kept doodling in my notebook.

"Why don't you call up some of your friends to go out for a coke? I'll let you take the car."

"I don't have any friends."

"You and the girls still on the outs?"

"That's putting it mildly."

"Cute and pretty as you are, I can't believe you have no one to pal around with. Why don't you ask Maylene McCord to get together and do something?"

"Oh sure. I'll do just that, first thing tomorrow morning."

At precisely what age do people get too old to understand anything?

Overnight, Indian summer took her leave. Monday was clear and chilly, with a pale new moon lingering in the morning sky, when I set out to walk to school. The exhilarating cold stimulated a glimmer of hope in me that I could change my life, although I didn't have a clue how.

I was waiting for the light to change at the intersection half a block from the house when a car horn honked. My father pulled up to the curb and waved like fury from his old Ford. Sick fear engulfed me.

"Hi, honey," he called out, leaning over and rolling down the window on the passenger side. "Want a ride to school?"

"No thanks. It's only two blocks."

"I got another job on a drilling rig." He held up two fingers for victory.

Pointing to the green light, I gave him a brief wave and said under my breath, "Hope you can stay off the sauce long enough to keep it."

With a discouraged smile, he drove on, and I was once again able to get a deep breath.

Della, Rhonda, and Faye were in our usual place when I got to school, but today, when they turned their backs on me, I got mad instead of hurt.

"Someday I'll run circles around all of you!" I cried.

"Take off!" Rhonda said with a smug laugh over her shoulder.

It was then that it came to me what I had to do.

CHAPTER 6
A Plan for Action

It wasn't going to be easy, but I had no choice. I couldn't spend the rest of my three years left in school as an outcast. On the way to first period in the band hall, I backed my ears and forced myself to speak to everyone I passed in the hall, popular or not. For encouragement, I kept a list, putting a star by each person's name who spoke back. In spite of their surprised looks, most everyone said "Hi." Those who didn't at least nodded. Gradually, instead of freaking me out, the process turned into a challenge to see how many in-crowd names I could star.

At the end of two days, I had five pages in my notebook filled with names. At least half had stars next to them, and at least a quarter were popular kids. Time to put my next ploy into action.

Maylene McCord, who played third clarinet, sat directly behind me in band. On day three, I twisted around in my chair to face her.

"Hi, Maylene."

She stopped combing her red ponytail long enough to flick glazed eyes over me before returning to the mirror in her compact.

"What did you think of the Elvis show the other night?" I asked.

Snapping the compact shut, she stood up and waved to Frances Latimer in the percussion section.

I turned back around and willed myself to vanish. It didn't work.

"Ask her again," my sensible voice said.

I turned back around, took a deep breath, and—lost my nerve.

"We couldn't have heard each other, anyway, over the screeching of instruments being warmed up," I said inaudibly to sensible.

"Never mind that other kids are chatting away," sensible replied in a sarcastic voice.

At break, I scurried out onto the fire escape where I wouldn't have to try. The in-crowd never went out there.

"I refuse to make a fool of myself," I said, this time out loud, to sensible.

"You're talking to yourself. Have your ex-pals driven you crazy?" a male voice said. I recoiled as Eugene Hoffmeyer stepped out with me and grinned.

"I could ask Rhonda out on a coke date. Maybe that would make them take you back."

I shrugged. "Do what you want to do. It doesn't matter to me anymore."

A frown creased his brows. "You look so lonesome these days."

His words stabbed into the shield of disinterest I kept wound around my public face. I was lonely. I felt fat, ugly, and totally unlovable.

I edged toward the door to go back inside. Better to look stupid failing to get Maylene's attention than to stare at his lovelorn face while he stripped down my walls.

"Oops, Mr. Nesbitt is tapping the old baton. See you later, Eugene."

"Julie, wait."

I turned, frowning.

"Would *you* go on a coke date with me?"

Why couldn't it be a cute boy begging me to go out? I didn't want to hurt him, but I didn't want to go out with him, either.

"Rhonda's already mad enough at me, Eugene. We'll both be better off if you ask her."

"She's just a Dilbert," he said, looking smug.

At least somebody on this earth didn't categorize me as one.

Instead of taking my usual seat at the back in Miss Isadora Bolenbaugh's, aka Miss Bowling Ball's, English class, I forced myself to take the vacant seat across the aisle from Maylene. She sat, scribbling frantically, her head bent over her notebook. Nerves rendered my lips too stiff to smile.

"Hi, Maylene."

She looked up with bright anticipation, saw me, and the smile beneath her freckled nose drooped.

I hated the way the tone slid downward when she said, "Oh, hi, Julie."

The dab of courage I had scraped up evaporated. How dumb could I be? Girls like Maylene McCord didn't talk to me.

Longing to fly out over the prison walls of school to some place where I would be instantly popular and cool, I turned my face away toward the window. Where was Elvis with all his palaver about confidence when I needed him?

Maylene's voice jerked me back to the classroom.

"I forgot to write my essay on Poe." Her famous green eyes with the yellow spots focused directly on me.

"It's not . . . due . . . uh . . . until tomorrow."

Her expression said she didn't think I knew which way was up.

"Miss Bolenbaugh said they were due on Thursday."

"That's right," I said. "Today is Wednesday."

Relief doused her face. "You have saved my life. I'm so bum-fuzzled."

I could tell she expected me to say something, but like always around popular kids, I'd been transformed into a mute. Frantic, I scoured my brain and, after way too long a pause, blurted, "Elvis Presley gave me a ride home the other night."

Her face went blank. "Do I know him?"

"The featured performer at the Free Hillbilly Amateur Show."

"Oh, *that* guy? Gave you a ride home? Hmmm. I'm surprised that you'd get in the car with a hood type like him."

Uh-oh, now she might think badly of me. But better that than not thinking of me at all.

"He's not really a hood. He just looks like one. Besides, Della and the others left me high and dry. He said if I weren't so young he'd take me to the party for him and his band." One minute I couldn't say a word, the next I was running off at the mouth.

Her mildly interested look lasted for about an eighth of a second before she turned back to her essay.

Once again, I rummaged through my mind to come up with something, anything to keep the conversation going. Then I remembered his picture tucked inside my zipper notebook.

"Look what he gave me."

She yanked it so hard from my hand I thought it would rip.

"'To my good luck charm,'" she read aloud. Her eyes popped. "Like crazy, like wow!"

Now I had her attention.

"This could be valuable if he were famous," she said.

"He might be, someday."

She made a face. "Nah, not with that greaseball look."

"He's already making records. He gave me one. 'It's All Right.'"

"You don't mean!"

"I play it every morning getting dressed. Drives Mama bonkers."

Her eyes studied me for the first time in recorded history.

"Did he take you straight home?"

"No, he took me to Old Hickory first, in his fabulous pink Cadillac."

"This gets better and better." She leaned toward me with a furtive face. "Did he . . . try anything?"

"Of course not. He was the perfect gentleman. We did dance, though."

"At Old Hickory? That is so cool! I am blown out of my tree. You know, it was really a lucky break that your friends went off and left you."

"I'll take that, if you please." Miss Bolenbaugh was standing over Maylene with her hand stuck out.

I froze. Maylene gave me a sick look.

"Right this very minute, young lady."

"It . . . it's not mine," Maylene stammered.

"All the more reason I should have it," Miss Bolenbaugh said, adjusting her corseted torso to a rigid posture in her brown-and-white flowered dress.

Throwing me an apologetic look, Maylene handed over the picture.

"Hmmm. Elvis Presley," Miss Bolenbaugh mused aloud, reading the signature on the glossy image. Her heavy Southern accent grew more pronounced. "I knew some Presleys once, over in Tupelo, where I was born and raised."

"That's him!" I exclaimed, forgetting myself.

"That is *he*," Miss Bolenbaugh said. "I take it you are the proud owner of this photograph, Miss Morgan?"

"Yes, ma'am."

"Here, put it away, and don't let me catch sight of it again."

I lowered my head. "No, ma'am."

The bell rang, and Maylene and I exchanged relieved looks as Miss Bolenbaugh banged on her desk to call the class to order.

In French class that afternoon, I managed to grab another seat next to Maylene. This time, miraculously, she spoke first.

"I didn't realize Miss Bolenbaugh was paying us a bit of attention in English class this morning."

"That woman has ears like a lynx," I said. "One time, before the bell for class, when everyone else was jabbering and making a huge racket, I whispered—whispered, mind you—to a friend next to me at the back of the room about how mad I was at Mama, and Miss Bowling Ball called out over all that noise, 'Julie, you shouldn't talk about your mother like that.'"

"Beats all, doesn't it? Listen, Julie, you always make good grades. Do you think French is hard?"

"Awful hard. And Mama doesn't call B a good grade."

Maylene leaned over and spoke in that confidential tone she always used with the in-crowd.

"My folks don't, either." She giggled. "Of course, I made a C. I hate conjugating verbs."

I nodded. "Me, too. And I hate all that Frenchie-baboo we have to listen to in the language lab."

Maylene sighed. "It might as well be Greek."

"Too bad it isn't," I ventured. "I can speak Greek—Sigma Chi."

First, she looked startled, and then she cracked up. "You fracture me! You're a wit, and I never knew it."

Amazed relief flooded me.

"I want to be Sweetheart of Sigma Chi when I get to college. Listen," she turned on the smile she was also famous for, "a bunch of us are getting together at Lynn Martin's tonight to study this Frenchie-baboo stuff. I love that! The girls would love to hear your tale about that Elvis guy. Want to come, too?"

CHAPTER 7
THE IN-CROWD

Mama came to me at my dresser that evening. "I'm so pleased Maylene McCord invited you to study French tonight." She took the brush from my hand and drew it through my hair. "You need to branch out, make more friends."

"Wonder how long the popular kids will tolerate Julie the Shy hanging around with them?" I said to her in the mirror.

"All you have to do is let them talk about themselves, and they'll adore having you around."

"How would you know?"

"I wasn't born in the dark ages." She laughed. "Seriously, though, never lose sight of who you are."

"Who am I, Mama?"

She lifted my chin with her finger and made me look at myself in the mirror.

"You are Julia Lawrence Morgan and able to hold your own with anyone. I know those girls' folks. Lynn Martin's mother and I were in the same sorority at the university. They're all nice people, but those girls don't have your bloodlines. My mother always told me that we are directly descended from the Murphys, who were kings of Ireland."

"Mama, have you lost your marbles? Don't say stuff like that."

"It's true. The blood royal flows in your veins, young lady."

"Oh right, and what would my father's contribution be to my *royal* blood?"

"Leave him out of this equation."

"I don't see how we can."

"I just mean, you're as good as those popular kids, and don't you forget it."

What I couldn't forget was that we were a broken family, with no man to change the light bulb on the porch or make us a living. Mama pounded a typewriter eight hours a day for barely enough money to keep food on the table and buy us clothes. And yet she could look down on other people. But I kept those thoughts to myself rather than spoil her illusion, which might be the last shred of dignity she had in this town, where a divorcée was a second-class citizen.

A horn honked in the driveway.

"That's Maylene!" I leaped up from the dresser stool and dashed to the front door.

"Bring the forty-five he gave you," Maylene called from the car.

I had the picture tucked under my arm, too, as I skipped down the porch steps and into the harvest-moon night.

All the way to Lynn's, Maylene chatted.

"You and I have known each other since kindergarten. We were in the same room in grade school every year. I wonder why we've never run around together."

I wanted to say "because you've never given me the time of day," but instead I asked, "Who all's going to be at Lynn's?"

"Frances Latimer and Laura Meade."

All the boys ogled Frances Latimer's boobs, no matter what she wore. Laura Meade was so short the boys called her "puppet," but she had lots of dates. I could hardly bear my excitement at the thought of being with them—or my anxiety that I might not be able to think of a word to say.

"Come on in," Lynn yelled from the front door.

Like ours, her house was a Southern bungalow. Maylene and I jumped out of the car and ran between the shadows of two oak trees lining the walkway.

"What's the tale, nightingale?" asked Laura when we were in Lynn's bedroom.

"Show them the picture, Julie," Maylene said, "and tell them what happened."

Lynn's mother appeared, carrying a tray of steaming mugs.

"I never heard such oohs and ahs and giggles," she said.

Lynn waved at her. "Hi, Mother. Bye, Mother."

"I brought you girls some hot cocoa."

"Thanks," we murmured in one voice.

"Julie, it's nice to see you included in this bunch of Giggling Gerties," she went on, looking for a place to set the tray. "How's your mother?"

"Fine."

"She never comes to Junior League anymore. She must work full time now."

"Yes, ma'am."

Mrs. Martin frowned. "Lynn, there's not a clear surface in this room."

"Here, I'll take it."

Lynn plopped the tray on the floor. Mrs. Martin scowled, then turned back to me.

"Your mother's a secretary for that big law firm in the bank building, isn't she?"

"Yes, ma'am."

"A college degree and she ends up having to type documents for those know-it-all lawyers. She could, no doubt, write them herself. Bet they don't pay her half what she's worth. What's the name of that firm?"

"*Mother!*" Lynn said. "Vamoose!"

"That doesn't sound like French to me. All right, I'm going back to the dope machine. Don't get too loud. Your sister's trying to study, too."

Lynn crossed herself and looked upward as her mother left the room.

"My mother calls the TV the same thing," I said. "She falls dead asleep the minute she sits down in front of it."

Lynn and I shared a huge handshake.

"Regale us with the Elvis Presley story," Maylene said.

"He's really nice," I began, sensing by the rapt silence that I had their full attention. They shared my trepidation about getting into the car with him. They couldn't believe the windows rolled up and down with a button. They squealed when I told them about dancing at Old Hickory with the autumn leaves fluttering down around us.

"I'm totally regaled," Frances Latimer said. "You had an El-venture!"

"Frances, you're hopeless," Maylene said. "Lynn, put the record on."

"Not too loud," called Lynn's mother from down the hall.

"We better be on guard," I warned. "With hearing that good, your mother could turn into Miss Bowling Ball."

They convulsed with laughter. Everyone had heard how a drip in her basement kept Miss Bolenbaugh awake all night on the third floor of her house.

Maylene patted my shoulder. "Good one, Julie."

I seem to be turning into a wit! Is the world coming to an end?

We played the record over and over. Oddly, in spite of how we felt about his long hair and sideburns, we couldn't help screaming when Elvis sang.

"Too bad he looks like a hood, Julie," Maylene commented.

"That doesn't matter," Laura said. "It's not like he's going to be at school every day to ruin her reputation."

"I'll clue you," Lynn said, lying back on a stack of pillows and entwining her fingers, "what razzes my berries about this whole story is that an older boy gave her a ride home. I can't wait to date older boys."

"Me too, me too," Laura squealed. "Don's older. Is it fun, Frances?"

Frances cut her eyes away. "He's just a year older, but still, you have to work a lot harder to keep your virginity."

"How are things with you and Don these days?" Maylene asked her.

"I thought he was on the verge of giving me his class ring, when he up and went out with *her*. I could kill her!"

"I should think you'd want to kill *him*," Lynn said. "He asked her out."

"She shouldn't have accepted." Frances took off her glasses and wiped her eyes. "I'm getting upset all over again."

"Julie, in case you haven't heard," Maylene said in a voice that sounded like somebody had died, "Don DeAngelo gave Frances the royal shaft and took Emma Jarvis to the movies last Friday night."

"Oh no!" I said.

"Oh yes, Emma Jarvis," Frances said, looking sick. "But he hasn't shafted me, Maylene, and I don't appreciate you saying that."

Laura reached over and squeezed Frances's hand. "Emma never lets anyone forget for a minute she was voted most beautiful last year."

"Keep your voices down," Lynn dropped into a whisper as she tiptoed to her bedroom door, took a quick peek out, and shut it again.

"Come on, y'all," Maylene said. "We've got to finish this French homework."

"I want some fresh input first," Frances said. "Julie, do you think I've been shafted?"

"Weeell," I began, remembering that Don and Emma were both a year ahead of us, "they are the same age."

"Oh God." Frances's face crinkled. "You *do* think I've been shafted."

"I bet you can get him back," I said, trying to sound upbeat.

"I bet you can, too," Laura said. "You're witty, and you have a great figure."

"You really think so?" Frances's voice pleaded for us to say "yes," and I did, but the truth was I couldn't imagine how any girl could get a boy back from Emma Jarvis.

"Every girl in school knows your motto—'Treat 'em rough and tell 'em nothing,'" I said. "Use it on him."

"I can't seem to do that when it comes to Donny." Her eyes brimmed.

"A girl simply has to know how to handle men," Maylene said, putting on a prim face.

Frances's eyes flashed. "You think I don't know how to handle men?"

"*Je ne sais pas.* It depends on how far you've already let Don go. A boy doesn't respect a girl who lets him go too far. He thinks she'll do the same thing with other boys."

"And the fact that you go with Steve Morton makes you an authority on boys?" Frances said. "The whole school knows he's light in the loafers."

"He is not!"

"Prove it," Frances said.

"Just because he's not always trying to feel me up?"

"Good ole, red-blooded American boys try to feel a girl up every chance they get," Frances said.

Lynn whispered, "It's not so bad, if it's only on top of your clothes."

"But you have to be careful," Frances said. "Once a boy gets in your pants, you go ahead and go all the way."

We burst into high-pitched giggles.

"My mother is going to hear you," Lynn hissed.

This discussion was the absolute *most*! The Della, Rhonda, Faye group would never in a million years talk about such things.

"We'd better do our French," Maylene said.

"Yes, let's *do* do good ole French," Laura said, "but first I have to ask Julie. Who was that woman wearing the gaudy earrings you were with at the stadium the other night?"

"I was with Della, Rhonda, and Faye, before they left me," I sputtered.

"But we all saw you walking out with some strange woman."

"That wasn't me." Heat crept up into my face. "Mama says she's probably a cousin umpteen times removed."

"Well, she must be your clone," Frances said with a wry face.

CHAPTER 8
The Camden Show

Studying with them for one night did not a member of the in-crowd make me. Days that seemed like weeks went by while they did no more than say "hi" or smile in the hall.

At school, I had no one to talk to or sit with at lunch. I had no one to call or go to the Dairyette with. Huddling even tighter at the flagpole before school—or at their lockers between classes—Della, Rhonda, and Faye only gave me smug looks.

To make things worse, I broke out with three pimples. I never had pimples! Fall humidity frizzed my hair. And Mama, with a hopeful smile, handed me a new bottle of mouthwash and said, "You just saw the dentist. It must be stress." I had become an untouchable with bad breath.

One day in November, when I was on the brink of crawling on my knees and begging my Dilbert crowd to take me back, Maylene tapped me on the shoulder in French class.

"Your boyfriend is doing a show tomorrow night."

Is she delusional? "What boyfriend?"

"That Elvis guy. He's playing in Camden. Wanna go with the gang? Or is he sending his pink Cadillac to carry you up?"

"I didn't know he was going to play in Camden," I said, half to myself.

"Some boyfriend he is!"

She tossed her head, and the tip of her red ponytail stung my cheek. I blinked, thankful it hadn't hit me in the eye.

"He's not my boyfriend, and he certainly hasn't made any plans to bring me to the show in the pink Cadillac or any other kind of car."

"But surely he'll remember you." Her tone implied that surely he would not. "So, are you going to make the scene and introduce us to him?"

If Elvis didn't remember me, I'd be nothing but bad news, but no way could I turn down an invitation from the in-crowd, or anybody, at this point. Maybe he *would* remember. After all, he was just another rockabilly with stars in his eyes.

I pinched myself to make sure I was actually with Maylene's crowd at the Elvis show and not asleep, dreaming.

He wiggled and shook, rattled and rolled. The girls in the audience screamed with every gyration, the five of us included.

"I like him so much better tonight," Maylene said as Elvis finished his final encore and moved to the front of the stage. "Come on, Julie. He's going to sign autographs down front. Introduce us."

The challenge in their eyes left me no choice but to edge into the throng waving one-page flyers for him to sign. Holding my breath and praying, I thrust mine into his hand.

"What's your name, honey?" he asked, his eyes focused on the paper.

Maylene's face broke into a satisfied smile.

Then, in a flash, my fortune changed. Elvis looked up at me, did a double take, and sputtered, "Juliet! You came all the way to Camden to see me!"

I was positive the dropping of Maylene's jaw made a palpable shock wave. Lynn, Frances, and Laura looked equally stunned.

"I came with my friends," I said, flushing with pride.

"I hope these aren't the friends who left you high and dry at the show in El Dorado," he said, "even though it did turn out to be my lucky night."

"No, these are new friends," I said and introduced them.

Elvis signaled the stage manager just behind his shoulder.

"Juliet, here, is my good luck charm. I'm going to take these ladies backstage for a coke."

Totally flipping out, the girls followed Elvis, with me on his arm, to his makeshift dressing room.

"He *does* know her," Maylene said under her breath.

"You better believe I do," Elvis tossed over his shoulder.

Maylene blushed but turned on the charm.

"Ell…vis," she drawled, "we really dig your music. The way you sing, you've got it made in the shade! Do you have a girlfriend?"

With a flick of an opener, he popped the cap off a frosted bottle of Coca Cola and winked conspiratorially at me.

"I would, if Juliet would have me."

"I guess he shot you down," Frances said, elbowing Maylene, whose lips were so tight they looked like a wrinkled prune. I held at bay the triumphant smile trying to take over my face.

Elvis and I played this backstage scene like we'd rehearsed it. Putting an arm around my shoulders, he spoke in a low, sexy voice.

"This is the last coke in my cooler, honey. Can we share it?"

I beamed.

"You can share mine," the girls chorused in one voice, each holding out her bottle to Elvis.

"One's enough," Elvis said, holding the last coke to my lips.

"We have to go," Maylene said, shifting into her persnickety mode.

"Want me to take you home?" Elvis asked me. "We're playing Texarkana tomorrow, and I can easily head out tonight and swing by El Dorado."

The girls' eyes squinted with envy.

"Thanks, but I promised Mama I'd come home with the gang."

"Always mind your mama," Elvis said. "She's the best friend you got. Y'all drive safe, now, ya hear? Juliet, you really are my good luck charm. I never had such a crowd, wanting autographs, before tonight. I just know it's all because you were here."

Maylene and the girls looked gaga as Elvis gave me a quick kiss on the cheek.

"Thanks for coming, y'all," Elvis said.

On our way out he called, "Don't forget me, Juliet. I'll remember you."

CHAPTER 9
THE DREAMSICLE

All the way home from Camden, the girls filled the car with a babble of chatter and gushing—over ME!

When they pulled into our driveway, Maylene said, "Julie, it might seem silly since you live only two blocks from the high school, but would you like to be in our carpool?"

"We can squeeze one more in," Frances said.

"You can keep us up to date on the big rock star," Lynn said with a chuckle.

"I'm beginning to think he really will be a star someday," I said.

Maylene nodded. "You just might be right. So do you?"

"You bet!" I said, giving them a thumbs up.

The next morning at eight fifteen sharp, a golden-throated horn sounded out front. Another popular member of the crowd, Darcy Doyle—a perpetually bouncy blonde with a great figure but the biggest boned girl alive—sat in the driver's seat of an orange-and-white, two-door car with glitzy chrome and tailfins that looked two feet long. Darcy's signature smile stretched almost to her ears.

"My folks got a brand-new car, and I get it on my days to drive the carpool! Isn't it a dream?"

"It's a Dreamsicle!" Frances Latimer quipped, unable to conceal the tinge of envy on her face.

"It is sooo cool, Darcy," I said, opening the passenger door.

Lynn leaned over as I pushed her seatback forward to climb in back with Maylene, Laura, and Frances, and we set off. I was still arranging my plastic, screen-wire petticoat when Darcy leaned on the horn to signal our arrival.

At the flagpole, Della, Rhonda, and Faye looked up. Their smiles drooped when they saw me get out of the car with Maylene's crowd. Things went downhill from there for my former chums.

"Get your food and sit with us," Della said, catching up with me on the way to the lunchroom that day.

You can't buy the revenge I got by giving her a brief smile and saying, "Thanks, but Maylene is saving me a seat."

"Julie, you should be careful of that crowd," Della said, stopping me with a warning hand on my arm.

"Oh? Why?"

"They aren't like us. They'll expect you to do stuff you won't want to do."

"Like what?" I demanded.

"Oh, stuff. Believe me, you're not like them. You've been brought up like we have. You should stick with your own kind."

"The last thing I heard from you and Rhonda and Faye was the silence of you all throwing me out of the group," I said. "For something I didn't do, by the way."

She looked hangdog. "I know what we did wasn't very nice," she looked into my face, "but I still believe you went out with Eugene."

"Well, that's your problem, isn't it? Gotta run now. Maylene's waiting."

A fine breeze blew that bright Friday as folks jammed the parade route from the stadium to the town square. Emma Jarvis, El Dorado High School's Homecoming Queen, riding atop a float of papier-mâché decorations, followed our ninety member band, spiffy in our new purple-and-white uniforms. A gasp went up when we topped the hill at the courthouse and burst into "The Stars and Stripes Forever." The applause and cheering shot a tingle up my spine that almost made my hair stand straight up and flip off my hat.

When the parade broke up, I found Mama in the crowd, standing with some of her card-playing pals.

"Maylene's invited the gang to her house for a party. Will you take my clarinet home?"

Mama laughed. "Thank God it's not a piano."

"Hurry up, Julie," Frances called from the group of girls waiting for me.

In my peripheral vision, I saw Della, Rhonda, and Faye watching me from the sidelines. We had shared so many dreams of being accepted into the popular crowd. Now I was in, and they weren't. No matter how great it felt to get even, a part of me was sorry they weren't included. And, like it or not, a part of me worried about Della's warning.

My sensible voice said, "Better be on the lookout for signs that what she said is true." But my daring voice said, "They're just jealous." Throwing the Dilberts a wave, I hooked arms with Frances and Maylene and danced off down the street, where Darcy was waiting for us in the Dreamsicle.

That day would have gone down in my diary as one of almost perfect happiness, except at that moment I happened to look over and see my lookalike staring at me from the crowd.

CHAPTER 10
I FORGOT TO REMEMBER TO FORGET

In early December, a package arrived for me in the mail.

"It's too soon for Christmas presents," Mama said as I brought it in from the porch, "and it's thin. Who would send you a package like that?"

I tore it open. Inside were a Christmas card and a forty-five record. "It's from Elvis!"

"What does it say?" Mama asked.

"Wishing you a Merry Christmas and a Happy New Year."

She wagged a finger. "No, what did he write?"

"That's none of your beeswax."

Up shot her eyebrow.

"Okay, okay, I'll read it.

Dear Juliet,

On November 21 I left Sun Records and signed with RCA. This is the biggest thing that's happened yet, and I wanted you to get the news straight from me. They rereleased this forty-five record under the RCA label. I know it's early to send a Christmas present, but I wanted you to have it to play for your friends. One of the songs describes exactly my feelings for you. You'll know which one.
Elvis

I pulled the forty-five from its sleeve. One side was titled, "Mystery Train." And on the flip side—"That's the one!" I said.

"The one what?" Mama asked.

"That describes his feelings for me. 'I Forgot to Remember to Forget.' Oh, Mama!" I clutched the forty-five to my chest and twirled around. "Finally, a guy likes me. I was beginning to think no one ever would."

"Eugene Hoffmeyer seems to like you," Mama said.

I scoffed. "He's such a klutz. None of the cute boys have the hots for me."

Mama shook her head. "It doesn't become you to use coarse language."

I sighed. "I'm not the lovable type, I guess."

"Darling, where did you ever get such an idea? Of course you're lovable."

I looked away from her. "Even my own father doesn't think so."

I cringed at the deeply concerned look that fell over Mama's face.

"Your father loves you, I'm sure."

"He doesn't even know me. Not really. I mean, who I am. He hasn't been around me enough."

"If he didn't love you, he wouldn't hound us all the time to see you."

"He loves the fantasy, who he *thinks* I am."

"Are you trying to tell me you want to see him more often?"

I looked away and mumbled, "I don't know what I want."

Her brow puckered, and her face took on a wounded look.

"I've tried to protect you from his drinking and his violent behavior by discouraging visits with him. I thought you dreaded them."

"I do. I've told you I don't want to ever visit him again."

"Do you remember the time . . . ?" She broke off.

"When he—"

"Don't talk about it!" Mama cried out.

I threw up my hands. "Jeez, you brought it up!"

"I know, and I shouldn't have. I can't talk about that little incident. It makes me too nervous."

"It was hardly a 'little incident,'" I said, blowing on my fingertips to warm them.

"It affects you, too," she said. "I can tell because your hands are cold. Your hands always get cold when you're nervous. Let's not discuss him. It only makes us unhappy."

I knew the subject was closed, and that was okay. What difference did it make if he didn't love me? I didn't love him. I didn't need him. I didn't want him in my life. I just couldn't seem to erase him from my mind.

"Anyway," I went on, "Elvis said he'd remember me, and he hasn't forgotten. He hasn't."

"He will," Mama said. "And Julie, you must forget him."

"Why? I'm his good luck charm, and he's my friend. And don't be so sure he won't make it. He's with RCA now. If you remember, our TV's an RCA."

During the Christmas holidays, I got some bad news from Maylene.

"Julie, it's all well and good that Elvis Presley sends you records and stuff, but the fact that you never get asked out on a date by a boy here in town makes people wonder why we're running around with you."

My arteries constricted.

"Your Dilbert status is still clinging to you like a bad smell, and it's threatening to rub off on us. You better get on the stick and get a flesh and blood boyfriend right here in El Dorado—pronto!"

"But who can I get? I wouldn't be caught dead with Eugene Hoffmeyer—even if he is the only boy on the planet who shows any interest in me."

She put her fingers to her temples and closed her eyes.

"A date with Eugene Hoffmeyer is better than no date at all. You don't have to go steady with him. Use him as a do-fer."

"A what?"

"A do-fer! He'll do fer now, until you can snag somebody better."

So the first week back to school after the holidays when Eugene asked me for the millionth time for a coke date after school, I caved.

The ride in his dead-grass green clunker, a 1941 Plymouth with no shocks, was brutal. Every bump in the road jarred the flesh like we'd hit a crater. Its wool seat covers scratched right through my clothes. How the mighty had fallen since the ride in Elvis's pink Cadillac. At least I knew how to open the door of the old Plymouth.

The Dairyette was a straight shot about five miles from my house. We were almost there when the Plymouth made a loud clunk and refused to go forward. Eugene's ears turned rouge-red.

"The transmission must have fallen out."

"What? I never heard of such a thing."

"Don't worry. I've got an idea."

Backing to the opposite side of the two-lane road, Eugene stuck his crew-cut head out the window and away we went, backward, due south.

"It's lucky we don't have to make any turns," he called over to me.

The speed with which news of our plight preceded us broke all records. People on the sidewalk gawked, pointed, and convulsed with laughter as we made our way, hind-part-before, along the town's main artery. Merchants and shoppers rushed from stores to see the spectacle. Ladies still hooked up to hair curling machines rushed out of Lucille's Beauty Parlor, dragging the contraptions behind them. Maylene, Frances, Lynn, and Laura flashed by, open-mouthed, as we sailed past the bookstore—backward.

Only in the in-crowd a few weeks, and I was ruined already!

CHAPTER 11
Heartbreak Hotel

On January twentieth, another package came from Elvis. Once again, it contained a forty-five record, this time accompanied by a note written on clean, white stationary.

Dear Juliet,

On January 27, 1956—mark it in your diary—RCA will release the song that I just know is gonna be my first hit—"Heartbreak Hotel." The flip side, "I Was the One," is good, too. I'm sending you a copy early, to impress the gang. Tune in to Stage Show Saturday, Jan. 28, on CBS. I'm going to be on TV for the first time! A network appearance! Scotty, Bill, and D.J.'ll be with me. It will be the biggest day in my life!

I'm enclosing an address for you to write me, if you want to.

Happy Ground Hog's Day—

Elvis

I put on "Heartbreak Hotel" and asked Mama, "How do you like it?"

With a worldly look in her eyes, she said, "I'm well acquainted with that hotel."

I was still on trial with the in-crowd, but I when I invited them to a party for Elvis's big night, they accepted with enthusiasm. As we all settled in around the TV on January twenty-eighth, my heart was racing.

"Tune in early," urged Maylene. "We don't want to miss a second."

"There he is! There he is!" Frances squealed.

Elvis plunged into "Shake, Rattle, and Roll," and we girls went ape, falling to the floor on our knees and screaming.

"He's obscene!" Mama said, rushing to the TV. "At least 'Your Hit Parade' won't destroy your morals."

"Don't change the channel!" I yelled, but she had already switched to Perry Como singing the number one song in the nation, "Hot Diggity." Pushing her aside, I flipped the switch back to Elvis.

"He's done it already!" I sang out.

"Done what? Destroyed your morals?" Mama cried.

"Got all girls screaming. He said he would."

"He's barely moving, Mrs. Morgan, compared to what he does onstage," Maylene said. "He won't destroy our morals. I promise."

In spite of her arched eyebrow, I could tell Mama was pleased that I was a mini-celebrity tonight with the in-crowd, and that Elvis Presley, now a national celebrity, was the reason for it.

"Tell you what, girls," she said, passing the platter of fudge, "if you want to call your folks for permission, I'll get out extra pillows and blankets, and we'll have a bunking party."

"Heartbreak Hotel" blared from the record player long after Mama went to bed at eleven o'clock.

"Won't this loud music keep your mother awake, Julie?" Laura asked.

"No, because she knows where we are."

"You know what?" Maylene said, sitting cross-legged on the floor. "I've decided that Eugene Hoffmeyer's not only sweet, he's cute."

"Then *you* go out with him," I said, wondering how much longer I could bear dating Eugene.

"You're hopeless," she said. "I should think you'd be glad you have a boyfriend."

"He's not my boyfriend."

"He's a hubcap, isn't he, Julie?" Frances said. "A boy who tries to be a big wheel but can't quite make it."

We cracked up.

"Let's make popcorn," I said.

In the kitchen Frances announced, "I've been saving this all night for a surprise, Julie."

I turned to her. "What?"

"I've come up with the perfect guy for you. Farrel Budrow. He's hip. I really dig him. And best of all, he and Don are good friends."

"I never heard of him. What year is he?"

"He's a college boy."

"Is he the dishwater-blonde guy you all were with at the hillbilly concert?" I asked.

"That's the one," Frances said.

I poured oil into a heavy pot, dropped three kernels in, and lit the stove.

"If this guy—Farrel—is off at college, what good would that do me?"

"He goes to Arkansas College, only thirty minutes away. Close enough to come home and take you out every weekend."

"Mama might think he's too old," I said.

"He's only nineteen. Elvis is twenty-one," Lynn said, closing her eyes and giving us her satisfied-cat smile.

"We'll help you work on her," Frances said. "He wants to transfer to the university in a year or two. If you could hook him, you'd be in fat city. I guaran-damn-tee-ya."

"Can we have butter on the popcorn?" Darcy asked.

"Oodles." I handed her a stick from the Frigidaire. "There's a little pan under the countertop to melt it in. Frances, there's not something weird about this Farrel person, is there?"

"No way, José. You've seen him. He's got great eyes, and he's tall and muscular, and like they say in that Shakespeare play we're reading in Miss Bolenbaugh's class, he's probably 'stuffed with honorable parts.'"

Maylene frowned. "Frances! You are so bad!"

Frances giggled. "I know it."

"And what's so great about Farrel's eyes?" Maylene asked. "Every time I see him, they're half shut."

"That's what makes him sexy," Laura said.

"Anyway, Julie, you two could double date with Don and me," Frances said. "Wouldn't that be fun?"

"*If* you ever get another date with Don," Maylene said.

"For your information," Frances said, preening, "I have another date with him tomorrow night."

"Tomorrow's Sunday," Maylene said. "Saturday is the important date night. Who's he out with tonight? That's the question."

"Jeez, Maylene!" Laura said.

In the band room yesterday, I had overheard Don say he had a date with Emma tonight. I focused on the popcorn, hoping Frances couldn't read my mind. I couldn't imagine what she saw in Don DeAngelo. Even though he made good grades, his deadpan expression made him look perpetually out to lunch. All he ever said was "Yep" and "Nope."

"Frances, does Don loosen up and talk when it's just two of you?"

"He talks with his hands. When we go to the drive-in, he never shuts up."

"You have to fight him off all during the movie?" I asked, shocked.

"Sure." Frances smirked. "I fight like a tiger." She put a hand on my shoulder. "This is one naïve child."

I wanted to go through the floor. Before I could say anything, the phone rang.

"Who on earth can be calling at this hour?" I said.

"Elvis!" they chorused.

My heart flip-flopped.

"Or Eugene," Maylene said.

"Shake the popcorn, somebody," I said, dashing to answer the phone before it woke up Mama.

It was my father. My insides twisted. I struggled to keep my face composed as they all stood watching me from the kitchen.

"I can't talk right now." A pulse pounded in my temple. "Do you know what time it is?"

Maylene hissed at me from the doorway. "It doesn't matter what time it is. You don't have a date for the Valentine dance. Accept him!"

"I have to go," I said. "I've got company."

"Don't hang up!" he said, raising his voice on the other end. "If you do, I'll come over there. Right now, tonight!"

I turned my back on the questioning eyes of the girls.

"Okay, tell me what you want before Mama wakes up."

"What'll she do, call the cops?" he said, slurring his words. "I want to see you, honey. Don't you want to see me?"

I didn't answer.

Not a sound came from the kitchen. The girls were listening to every word. For a long minute, there was only silence on the other end. Just as I decided he'd passed out, he said something that scared the hooty out of me. Without a word, I hung up on him and went back into the kitchen.

"Did you melt the butter?" I asked, avoiding their eyes.

"Couldn't find the pan," Darcy said, dumping the puffy kernels into a bowl.

I got the pan and handed it to her.

"You're trembling," Laura said, taking hold of my chilly fingers. "What did he say to upset you so?"

"Nothing."

Lynn looked at me with questioning eyes. "Was it Eugene?"

I didn't answer. Curiosity blazed on all their faces.

Darcy gasped. "It was *Elvis!*"

Laura let out a shriek.

"Don't wake up Mama," I said.

"You sounded cross with him," Laura said. "You didn't even tell him how good he was on TV."

"It couldn't have been Elvis," Maylene said. "She wouldn't have used that tone with him."

Frances studied me with suspicious eyes. "That wasn't Elvis or Eugene, was it?"

My attempts at staying cool crashed and burned. "No, actually it wasn't."

"Where are you going?" Maylene asked, following me out of the kitchen.

"To lock the doors."

"Why?" Laura asked. "Is something wrong?"

"No, we just lock our doors at night. That's all."

They exchanged uncomfortable looks.

I forced a carefree tone into my voice. "Come on, let's eat the popcorn."

"By the way, Frances," Maylene said, "you aren't the only one that's been sitting on a surprise. I was in the school office yesterday, and guess who I saw?"

"Who?" We chorused.

"Julie's lookalike, registering for school."

CHAPTER 12
FARREL BUDROW

On Thursday before the Valentine dance, I was on my way to the band room when someone called out from behind me.

"Carmen, here are the results of your test for placement in a foreign language class."

I walked faster. Rushing footsteps caught up and someone tapped my shoulder.

"Carmen!"

I whirled around. Mrs. Burton, the guidance counselor, stared at me in disbelief.

"Julie? I can't believe it! I thought you were the new girl. Have you met her yet?"

I could barely breathe.

"If you see her, tell her I have her test results."

"Is she going to be in my French class?" I asked, trying to sound like a nice girl instead of one that would like to see Carmen dragged back to wherever she came from by a flock of demons.

Mrs. Burton smiled. "No, she's taking Spanish. That's so sweet of you, though, to be willing to welcome her to our school."

"Oh but—," I began, but she was already bustling on down the hall, her nylons swishing with every step.

I stormed up to the band room and sprawled in my chair.

"Who rattled your cage?" asked Maylene.

"Mrs. Burton mistook me for Carmen."

"Oh no!" Maylene's hand flew to her mouth.

"What am I going to do?"

"This is getting serious," Maylene said. "If only she didn't look so—"

"Cheap?" I said.

Maylene nodded. "And so much like you. Oops! I don't mean you look cheap." She laid her fingertips against her cheeks, which had turned quite red. "Let's hope she doesn't get elected Valentine queen the first month she's in school. That would really be trouble. Listen, Julie, I have to ask you. Who was that who called the other night when we were at your house?"

I frantically tried to conjure up a lie.

She patted my arm. "You can tell me. We're friends."

I had pushed that conversation with my father to the back of my mind, hoping he had been so drunk he wouldn't remember the next day.

"You don't have to tell me, if you don't want to," she babbled on. "I respect your privacy. But just tell me this. It wasn't some cute boy you haven't told us about, was it?"

"No, Maylene. It wasn't some cute boy."

On the way to Frances's car after the last bell that day, she gathered us into a huddle on the campus lawn.

"Big news!" She held out a ring on a chain around her neck. "Ta-da!"

"Don's senior ring?" Darcy cried, her grin smacking her ears. "Oh Frances, that's wonderful!"

"When did this happen?" Maylene asked

Did I detect a tinge of displeasure in Maylene's tone?

"At my locker a few minutes ago." Frances's smile was like spring sunshine. "We had a date last night, you know."

"You're so calm," Laura said. "I'd be running around, screaming it all over the place."

"A girl has to play it cool," Frances said.

Maylene flipped her pony tail. "But he had a date with Emma only the night before."

"Emma is history. Don and I are officially going steady. And guess what else?" She leaned into the circle and whispered, "He said he loves me."

"That's great, Frances," I said. *What kind of trap had she sprung to get him back?*

"Hey, you all." Darcy waved both hands to interrupt. "I have an announcement, too. Larson Mullaney, who, as you know, is the absolute most, asked me for a date to the Valentine's dance!"

"Like crazy, like wow!" Maylene said. "He's a doll."

As we navigated toward Frances's car, I saw Carmen getting into a dented Chevy with peeling mauve paint. The woman with the dangling earrings sat at the wheel, smoking. Both she and Carmen stared as we passed.

"Lookee. There she is," Maylene said.

I grabbed her hand. "Don't point."

"Dibs on the front seat," Laura and Darcy cried, crawling into the car.

"You could at least let us get in first," Maylene said as we crawled in back. "We have to find out who she is."

Laura looked over her shoulder at us. "But how?"

"It's simple," Maylene said. "Make friends with her."

Frances's skeptical face reflected in the rearview mirror. "Yeah, but then we might get stuck with her."

"The way she dresses, she probably won't want to run with us," Laura said.

"Don't kid yourself," Frances said. "Everybody wants to run with us."

"Not everybody," Laura said.

Frances chuckled. "Name just one who doesn't."

Silence fell.

"Kids in New York?" I ventured.

Laughter rocked the car.

"Whoopee!" Frances cheered. "Chalk one up, girl. You're always so serious. Come to think of it though, that's why I like you. You're a drop of intelligence in a sea of mindless giggling." She turned the car in the direction of the Dairyette. "And I bet you think we can do without Maylene's bright idea."

"I don't want to seek her out. I'd rather wait until we're thrown with her," I said. "Sooner or later, we'll find out who she is."

Maylene poked me. "I don't understand why you aren't more curious. I am."

I shrugged.

"We should hook her up with good old Eugene," Frances said. "That would get him off your back."

"Eugene's nice," Maylene said.

"But there's no current demand for nice boys," Laura said.

"You'll land a decent guy any day, Julie, now that you're running with the right crowd," Frances said.

I reached over and patted her shoulder. "Thanks."

We pulled into the Dairyette parking area, and before Frances could switch off the motor, the college boy sauntered toward us.

"Farrel!" Frances said as he stuck his head in the window on the driver's side. "What are you doing here? Aren't you supposed to be in school?"

"We had today off. I have to go back tonight."

He smiled a lazy smile while his lidded gaze roamed through the car and came to rest on me. Our eyes met, and my heart stopped. We'd just read the line "Whoever loved that loved not at first sight?" today in English class. Now I knew what it meant.

"Am I seeing double?"

He glanced over his shoulder. About five cars away from us sat the dented, mauve Chevy, with Carmen and the woman in the front seat.

"That's Julie's lookalike," Frances said. "Julie Morgan, meet Farrel Budrow."

"Glad I don't need to see the eye doctor," he said, grinning at me.

"Get in back," Frances ordered, pulling her seatback forward and throwing me a gleeful look.

I slid closer to Maylene to make room for him. His long legs forced his knees against the front seat.

"Scoot up a little, Frances," he said, giving me another smile.

The faint smell of his aftershave made me lightheaded.

"Where've you been all my life?" he asked, looking down at me.

"Lost in Nowheresville," Frances said.

Maylene leaned around me to look at Farrel. "We rescued her."
Could life get any better?

"Did you meet that girl over there?" I nodded toward the mauve Chevy.

"No, I just noticed her when I got my coke. Want a sip?"

A tingle ran through me when his fingers, chilly from holding the icy cup, brushed against mine. I loved the way his dishwater-blond hair fell on his forehead.

"Farrel, are you coming home for the Valentine's dance?" Frances asked.

"When is it?"

"Easter weekend." She shrieked with laughter.

"Come on, Frances," he said.

"It's this coming Saturday, the eleventh," I told him.

"I was just seeing if Farrel was awake," Frances said. "Don and I are going. Have you heard the latest?" She held the ring out for him to see.

"I'll have to send Don my condolences," Farrel said. "I can hear his shackles rattling clear out here at the Dairyette."

"Farrel!" exclaimed Frances. "That's awful. You ought to get yourself a girl. There's nothing like having a steady you can love and count on."

"I'll give it some thought. And if I'm able to come home for the dance, I'll swing by."

"Why don't you get a date," Maylene said, leaning around again.

"You available?" he asked her.

"No, I'm going with Steve."

He snapped his fingers. "Shucks, I'm always a day late and a dollar short when it comes to you, Maylene. Darcy, Laura—y'all got dates yet?"

"We both do," Laura said.

"You could take Julie," Frances said.

I wanted to sink through the floor of the car until Farrel, his slow eyes boring into mine, said, "I can't believe *you* don't have a date."

I willed myself not to blush. It didn't work.

"Give me your number," he said. "If it looks like I can get back, I'll call you."

I wanted to jump out of the car and whirl, dancing all around the Dairyette parking lot. Instead, I fished in my purse for a pen.

Taking the torn slip of paper, he threw me a wary look.

"There's not some big, bruiser boyfriend in the picture that'll clean my clock, is there?"

"You're safe," I said.

"Good deal. Let me out, Frances. Curiosity is killing this cat. If I'm going out with Julie here, I need to find out who that girl is that looks like her. Hurry up, before they drive off."

That girl again!

By the time he got his long legs out of the car, the mauve Chevy was pulling away. Farrel stuck his head back in the car window.

"Like I said, always a day late and a dollar short." He winked at me. "Maybe that won't be the case with you, huh, Julie."

CHAPTER 13
DESPERATE AND DATELESS

Mama sat, lounging in her easy chair, sipping a cup of coffee, when I got home the next afternoon. I threw my books on one of the red corduroy couches and gave her a peck on the cheek.

"It's five thirty. Where've you been?"

"The Dairyette. Has anyone called?"

"Yes . . ."

"Was it Farrel Budrow?"

"That's a name I haven't heard."

"He said he might call me for a date to the Valentine's dance this Saturday."

"How gentlemanlike." Mama looked heavenward. "It's already Thursday. At any rate, it wasn't he who called."

"Then who?"

"One of my favorites." She beamed a self-satisfied smile.

I threw myself onto a couch, crying "Nooo! Not Eugene Hoffmeyer, again!"

"Yes, dear Eugene. He asked me if you had a date to the dance, and I said not to my knowledge."

"Oh no!"

She looked pleased with herself. "I was sure you'd be happy to have him take you."

"You told *him* that?"

"Well." She looked sideways at me. "In so many words."

I folded my arms across my chest.

"Eugene Hoffmeyer is a wet rag. I refuse to go to any more dances with him."

"I know his parents. They're nice people. It wouldn't be polite to turn him down." Donning her snob attitude, Mama picked up her china cup with a curled pinky. "Besides, it's already Thursday, and the dance is Saturday. This Farrel something—"

"Budrow."

"Is late on the uptake. For a date to the dance, he should have called at least a week ago."

"He didn't know me a week ago. I just met him yesterday. Besides, your 'dear' Eugene only called today."

Mama raised an eyebrow. "How could he not have known you a week ago?"

"He's off at school."

"Off?"

"In college."

"Where? Arkansas College?"

"How did you know?"

"I guessed as much, if he's back home so often."

"I've already said I'd go with him, if he calls. It wouldn't be polite to turn him down, either."

Mama let out a quick breath of exasperation and closed her eyes.

"Julie, Julie, Julie. 'If he calls.' Haven't you more pride than that?"

I shrugged and looked out the window into the wintry backyard.

"If he doesn't call, you won't have a date to the dance."

I thought of Maylene and my shaky position with the in-crowd. This dance might mark the end for me if I didn't have a date.

"If Farrel calls by tonight, can I go with him?"

Mama sighed. "How much older than you is he?"

"Weeell, I'm not sure. He's a freshman in college. Just four years."

"*Four years*? Absolutely you are not going out with him! And that's *final*."

"Mama! You, yourself, have said, when you get older, age doesn't matter."

"If you want to go to the dance, call Eugene back and accept him."

I got up and stomped out to the living room. Mama followed right on my heels, and that made me so mad that, right then and there, I decided, if Farrel did call, I'd defy her and meet him at the dance.

"Looking for the mail?" she said. "It's on the commode."

With one hand on my hip, I turned, shaking my head in despair.

"Mama, that's gross. Please don't say that in front of my friends. Can't you call it a hutch?"

She gave me a lofty look. "That piece of furniture was correctly called a commode all the way back to the days when your great-great-grandmother had it shipped up the river from New Orleans. It remains so today."

She really was hopeless.

On top of the stack of mail lay an envelope addressed to me. I tore it open. A heart-shaped card read, *A Valentine for Someone Special. Though miles lie between us and keep us apart, thoughts of you linger each day in my heart.* At the bottom was handwritten, *To my good luck charm! Elvis.*

"I'm out of my tree!" I clutched it to my heart.

"There's something else for you," Mama said. "From your father."

"How do you know it's from him? Did you open it?"

"The return address."

I ripped it out of the envelope. "It's a valentine, too."

"Let me see it," she said.

I held it out of her reach. "It's mine."

She wrested it from me and read, "Remember what I said the other night."

I snatched it back.

"What's he talking about?" Mama demanded.

"I guess he's decided it's time for a visit," I said, stuffing it back into the envelope.

"Have you been talking to him?" she asked.

I cowered in the face of her stern expression.

"He called the night the girls stayed over, that's all."

"Why didn't you tell me?"

"I *am* telling you."

She bristled.

I didn't dare tell her before, given what he said.

Her voice ratcheted up a decibel. "Don't give me a smart answer like that."

"You were asleep, and he was drunk. I figured he wouldn't even remember calling the next day."

"Is that all he said?" she asked. "That he wanted to see you?"

"Un-huh."

Taking me by the chin, she scrutinized my face. "Are you telling me the truth?"

"Yes!" I jerked my chin away and took off for my room. "I have to do my homework."

"You'll need your books, I imagine."

Her face said she knew I was hiding something.

Slumping, I turned, and under her parental gaze, I scuffed back to the den to get them.

Even though I sent Farrel ESP messages, he didn't call that night. In fact, he didn't call at all. By Friday morning, it was the consensus of the carpool that I should accept Eugene.

CHAPTER 14
The Valentine Dance

On the night of the dance, Eugene came to the door dressed in a white sport coat and bearing a small box of flowers. Mama watched, beaming, as he took out the corsage and fumbled with the pin stuck in the backing.

"Let me pin it on," he said and moved toward me, lust pulsing in his eyes. The next second the palm of his hand was resting on my breast.

"Jeez Louise!" I yelped, jumping backward.

"Julie!" Mama said. "What's the matter with you? Let Eugene pin on the corsage."

"Dream on." I snatched the flower and the pin and did it myself.

"That was pretty sneaky," I said, as he started the car and pulled away from the curb.

He turned fake-innocent eyes on me. "What was?"

"Using the corsage as a cover for feeling me up."

"I was just bracing my hand so it wouldn't shake. Besides, how else am I going to get a feel?" He twisted one end of an imaginary moustache.

"You are disgusting."

He cackled. "How do you like this car?"

"At least it goes forward."

"It's my father's, and I know, it's just a plain old car. Someday I'll have a white convertible with a blue ragtop, leather seat covers, and an automatic transmission. Then will you let me . . . uh . . . pin your corsage on?"

"No. Keep your hands off me."

"Julie, you're so weird."

"*I'm* weird?"

"I bet you'd go steady with me, if I asked you, but I'm not asking."

I shook my head in despair.

Paper hearts and cupids trailing red and white streamers decorated the enormous room used for dances at the teenage club, aka the TAC House. There was nothing as blatant as a sign on our table reading "In-Crowd Only," but other kids knew better than to try to sit there.

"Wow! I'm moving up in the world," Eugene said as we took the two remaining seats at the end closest to the dance floor. I cringed.

Across from us, perpetually effervescent Darcy bubbled over Larson Mullaney. Next to them, Laura Meade and her date watched Darcy in disbelief. Beside me, Maylene and Steve behaved like a bored married couple, while Don and Frances played "kissy face" down at the far end.

At a table on the opposite side of the dance floor, Della, Rhonda, and Faye sat with their dates, boys who still played tag on the school grounds during the lunch break. Rhonda glared at Eugene, while Della's and Faye's faces wrinkled as if they'd swallowed castor oil at the sight of me within the sacred folds of the in-crowd. Thank God they didn't know how shaky my position was.

The local DJ from KDMS radio station fired up the music. The dimmed lights remained bright enough that teachers and parents vigilantly chaperoning would not miss any hanky-panky taking place on the dance floor.

A new dance, the Push, brought home at Christmas by students at the University of Arkansas, was the current craze. Most everyone had it down pat, except Eugene, who moved like a floundering walrus.

"You'd think the chaperones would love this new dance," he said, his foot crunching down on my toe, "since it keeps us at arms-lengths."

I writhed in pain and sidestepped out of the way as he slung me under his arm.

"They're saying it's as vulgar as Elvis's gyrations," I said, "which is so silly. His slightest move drives the old folks bonkers."

"None of his moves are slight," he said, yanking me toward him.

"Jeez," I shouted over the music, "are you trying to pull my arm out of its socket?"

He swung me around again. I landed facing Della, Rhonda, and Faye's table. I loosed my hand from Eugene's grip and stood still.

"What's the matter?"

"Look there," I said, turning so my back was to their table. "Behind me."

Carmen had arrived and was sitting with them without a date and wearing a dress the color of Red Hots.

Eugene laughed. "Where are you, Julie—on the dance floor with me, or over there with them?"

I might have been more upset at the sight of her, had Eugene not jerked me under his arm again at precisely the right moment for me to land face to face with Farrel Budrow sauntering in. His eyes swept first over me, then Eugene. A brief smile twitched the corner of his mouth. Moving on, he made his way past the dancing couples to our table and pulled up a chair next to Don and Frances.

At least I had a date, even if he was a walking flake. I avoided Farrel's eyes when, breathless, Eugene and I flopped down in our chairs, but in my peripheral vision, I saw him flick a wave to me.

Maylene leaned over and whispered, "Farrel's here. You aren't going to cry, are you?" She actually looked like she hoped I would.

"Cry? Why would I cry? He never said for sure he'd call."

"Good girl," she said, patting me on the shoulder.

I hated when she did things like that. Taking a sip of my watered-down coke, I fought with myself to keep from looking at Farrel. A few minutes later, I lost the battle and stole a quick glance at him. He sent a smoky-eyed stare back to me from the shadows on his end of the table.

"Dance?" he mouthed.

Hating myself, I nodded. Maylene and the crowd looked big-time pleased as I went to meet him on the dance floor.

The top of my head came up to his collarbone as he pressed me close. Elvis's "I was the One" blared from the speakers. I felt a light kiss on the top of my head.

"Sorry I didn't call," he said.

A thrill undulated through my body. I pulled back a little to look at him.

"Oh, right. You did say something about calling. I completely forgot. I've been so busy lately."

His lips formed another of those ever so slight smiles.

"Is that your boyfriend you're with?"

"No, he's my *pest*."

Farrel laughed and drew me close again. I stuck out my behind.

"Doing an A-frame for the chaperones?" he asked. "Or for me?"

"Both," I said, blushing.

His aftershave made me giddy. I didn't dare ask what it was. He'd think I was completely gone over him already. Which I was.

Eugene tapped Farrel on the shoulder and stepped between us. "My turn."

"Later gator," Farrel whispered into my ear.

"Who is that jerk?" Eugene demanded, clinching a fist. "He's cruisin' for a bruisin'."

"And who's going to give it to him?"

"Me."

"You and what army?"

Breaking away from Eugene, I flounced back to the table, straight to the empty chair next to Farrel.

Eugene glowered as I leaned against Farrel's arm resting on the back of my chair.

"Want a sip?" Farrel asked, passing me his coke. He bent forward, letting his hand slip to caress the back of my neck. "Hey, Don, you on for poker tomorrow night? Hammy Gunther's getting up a game at his Calion lake house." He leaned back again and turned his slow eyes on me. "I'd take you with me, but no women allowed."

"I have other plans, anyway," I said, remembering to play it cool. "But sometime I'd like to learn to play poker."

Farrel moved his hand from the back of my neck. "Here comes your date."

Panting, Eugene rushed up to us. "Julie, that girl that looks like you wants me to take y'all's picture together."

"Why?"

He shrugged, palms up. "Because you look so much alike, I guess."

"I don't want to."

Farrel put his hand on my knee. "Aren't you curious about her?"

I bit my lip. I didn't like having someone around who looked so much like me. I wished she would dematerialize, vanish, as quickly as she had arrived on the scene.

"Julie," Maylene called to me from down the table, "get your picture made, and let's get the real skinny on this girl. I'll go with you."

"Go on," Farrel said, rubbing my shoulder.

I looked deep into his eyes. "You really think I should?"

"I think it'll be a gas."

So I got up and went with Maylene and Eugene across the dance floor to that other table.

CHAPTER 15
THE REAL SKINNY

At their table, Della and Faye turned sulky faces on Maylene and me, while Rhonda stared at Eugene with pooling eyes.

With our symmetrical, square-shaped faces, our slightly tilted noses and high foreheads, it was easy for people to mistake Carmen and me for each other. Even our eyes were the same color, cerulean blue, although hers reflected a worldly-wise look that mine did not. Falling halfway down her back, her hair was the exact same auburn color as my chestnut bob that stopped at my shoulders. Basically, that was the only difference anyone could see, right off.

I hung back, but Maylene walked right up to her and stuck out her hand.

"I'm Maylene, and your lookalike here is Julie."

Carmen got up from her chair. "I've been wanting to meet you."

I forced a half-smile. "It's wild that we look so much alike."

Eugene, now hanging over Rhonda's shoulder, took the Brownie Hawkeye camera Carmen held out to him.

"Now y'all stand close together," he said. "I want to make sure I get both your pretty dresses." Stepping back to focus, he stumbled and crashed into the next table. "Do-do hole," he yelped.

With darting eyes, he looked around. "Hope nobody heard that."

"Only everybody," I said, cringing.

Carmen and I put our arms around each other's waist. Her Red Hot dress looked like it had been made over for her. The overall effect of the too-short skirt, edged with fraying net, and the top, cut way too low for a teenager, could be summed up in one word—slutty.

My pale-blue silk dress with spaghetti straps and pleated skirt flared in waves when I whirled in my flat-heeled shoes. It wasn't expensive, but it didn't make me look cheap. It looked like what it was, a party dress for a teen.

"Get closer," Maylene told Eugene, "or their faces will be too small."

The flash went off. I blinked to clear away its harsh ghost floating in my eyes.

"Shall we skedaddle?" I asked Maylene under my breath. "I'm getting frostbite from my old 'friends.'"

"We haven't gotten the real skinny on this girl yet," she whispered back.

Eugene flopped into an empty metal chair and patted the one next to him.

"Julie, sit here by me. Maylene, pull up a chair for yourself."

"Talk about a Dilbert," Maylene said, loud enough for everyone to hear.

"We need to get back to our table," I said.

"I brought you to this dance," Eugene said. "You should stay with me."

"Sit down with us for a minute," Carmen urged.

"The DJ's still on break," Maylene said, dragging a chair from the next table. "At least we can talk a few minutes without screaming." She scooted in and said to Carmen, "I'm dying to find out how you two could possibly look so much alike. Julie says you might be kin."

"If we are, I don't know about it," Carmen said.

"What is your last name?" Maylene asked her.

"Newton, as in Sir Isaac, only my daddy didn't discover gravity," Carmen said. "He's in the military. Do you have any Newtons in your family, Julie?"

"Not a one. Maylene, we'd really better get back."

But Maylene pressed on with Carmen. "Are your folks from here?"

"Mother's family is, but my dad is from Minnesota. He was on his way to Fort Polk in Louisiana—he's a military man—when he met Mother at the bus station. They got married three weeks later."

"Love at first sight," I murmured and stole a look across the room at Farrel. He was not looking at me.

The DJ came back inside from his cigarette break, and "Roll with Me, Henry" nearly blew out our eardrums. Farrel led Darcy to the dance floor. If I'd been sitting over there, instead of here trying to find out about a girl I never wanted to meet anyway, it might be me on the dance floor with him.

"You've probably seen Mother picking me up at school," Carmen said, "in that broken-down Chevy of Grandma's. We hate that old wreck."

"Bet it beats mine," Eugene said, laughing at his attempt at a joke.

"So how come you and your mother and dad are back here in El Dorado?" Maylene asked, leaning toward Carmen.

"My dad is still over in Germany, where he's stationed, but Grandma broke her hip, and Mother came back to take care of her. I have to help, too, because Mother just got a job as a nurse at Warner Brown."

"Wow," Eugene said, "Germany! I want to go there someday. My ancestors came from there."

"The military has sent us all over the world," Carmen stated matter-of-factly.

In spite of all that travel, Carmen didn't seem any more sophisticated than the rest of us, who hadn't been anywhere.

"Enough about me," she said. "Tell me about you, Julie."

"There's nothing to tell," I shouted over the music.

The song ended, and Farrel asked Laura Meade to dance. I forced myself to look away as a slow song started and he pulled her close.

"There must be something," Carmen said.

Her pressing questions felt like an invasion of my private self. I ran my fingers over the bumps in the milk glass budvase on the table.

"Have you always lived in El Dorado?" she asked.

"Born and raised, and I've never been anywhere else."

"Except on band trips to Little Rock and Shreveport," Eugene said.

"And to Camden," Maylene added, moving the budvase out of my reach. "I'll tell you something about Julie. She's Elvis Presley's girlfriend."

My leg began to jiggle. "No, I'm not. He gave me a ride home the night of his concert. That's all there was to it."

"Wow!" Carmen's eyes widened. "How did that happen?"

I looked straight at Della, Rhonda, and Faye. "My so-called friends went off and left me."

Della, Rhonda, and Faye looked sick.

"Don't let her kid you," Maylene said. "Elvis gave her his picture, and he sends letters and records. He even sent her a valentine."

"That is so cool," Carmen said.

Gloomy-faced Eugene plucked at the flower now wilting on my shoulder.

"I gave her this."

"He's gotten famous since that concert," Carmen said. "'Heartbreak Hotel' is at the top of the charts. They say he might make a movie. Who's your favorite movie star, Julie?"

Stop the quiz! I took a deep breath and ordered myself to be patient. "Paul Newman." My eyes wandered back to Farrel and Laura on the dance floor.

"Mine, too," Carmen's eyes sparkled. "And your favorite subject?"

What would this girl ask next? "Band."

"I love music, too. And what does *your* dad do?"

Dong. Here we go. My chest constricted. I fought against saying that most of the time he does nothing but drink.

"Oil rigs," I mumbled. "He works on drilling rigs."

The music stopped. Laura went back to her chair, and then, a miracle. Farrel walked straight toward our table.

"Hi everybody," he said, looking only at me. "Dance, Julie, before I have to hit the road?"

I sprang to my feet and moved to him.

"But—" Carmen began.

"Get me away from here," I said to Farrel under my breath.

He took my hand with a touch that made my insides quiver.

"I'll have a copy of the picture made for you," Carmen called out as the opening bars of "Heartbreak Hotel" filled the room and Farrel led me to the dance floor.

CHAPTER 16
Sweeter Than Wine

Easter Sunday was on April Fool's Day that year. Darcy, Frances, Maylene, and I kept on our Easter dresses all day and even wore them that night when Mama let me have the car to go to the show.

At the Dairyette after the movie, Farrel, Don, Larson Mullaney (Darcy's heartthrob), and Justin Moore (another senior), squeezed into the car with us. Farrel got in next to me, sliding the seat back to make room for his legs behind the wheel. Within seconds, he suggested that we play Cockeye.

"What's that?" I asked.

"You'll like it," he said with a sly smile. "Here's the deal. If one of you girls sees a 'cockeye' first—a car with only one headlight—you each get to slap us guys. Buuut . . ." he drew out the word, building suspense, "if a guy sees one first, we each get to kiss all you girls. Sound like fun? Look. Here comes one. Cockeye!"

Taking me in his arms, Farrel laid a kiss on me that sent me reeling. Then he reached for Maylene, while Justin did a contortion act around them to give me a smooch. In the back, Don and Larson were busy with Frances and Darcy. By the time each guy had kissed each girl, we were a tangled mess of bodies and screen-wire petticoats.

It didn't take us long to abandoned the slapping aspect of the game and give over entirely to kissing. Don's mouth pressed my lips so hard my teeth cut into them. Larson left a ring of spit around my mouth that I had to surreptitiously wipe off. Justin's kiss gave my heart a quick flutter, but Farrel's kiss—not too wet, not too dry, not too gentle, not too hard—was perfect.

Don suggested that we leave the Dairyette and go to the woods.

"I'll drive," Farrel said, and headed north on Highway 7.

He switched on the radio, and Elvis's mellow voice filled the car with "I Was the One." Our arms touched as we flew along the road. I studied his profile. He wasn't handsome, but his jaw was strong and his smile, engaging. About three miles past Old Hickory, he turned onto a narrow, gravel road.

"This'll be nice and quiet," he said, switching off the engine in a spot where we could still see cars on the main highway.

We stuck with the game for one more cockeye, but after that, Farrel kissed me and simply didn't move on to the next girl. The others got the message and also paired off.

Darcy and Larson stayed in the car with Farrel and me.

"We're going to stretch our legs," Maylene said, and she and Justin got out and walked around nearby where we could see them. Don and Frances got out too, but they strolled into the woods out of sight.

Farrel's kisses made me weak, faint, and wild—like Elvis's music. My sensible voice mentioned that kissing so passionately might not be a good idea, but my daring voice said, "Enjoy it." I figured I might as well, given there was no way I could resist. He surely couldn't kiss me like this if he didn't like me a lot.

We were practically lying on the seat, and his hand was inching too close to the upper area "forbidden zone," when a tap sounded on the window. We jerked apart and sat up. Maylene stood, watching us with a schoolteacher face.

"Julie, I've got to get home. It's after eleven, and we can't find Don and Frances."

"They're down in the woods," Farrel said. "We'll give 'em a honk."

My face burned under Maylene's reproving gaze. I had been about to stop Farrel's roving hand myself when she caught us, but of course, she didn't know that. She kept me in knots about my shortcomings. Either I didn't have a cute boyfriend or it looked like I was about to let one go too far.

"The sky is glorious with stars," Farrel whispered to me.

"You're a poet," I said.

"I am when it comes to stars. Let's make a wish on one."

"I wish—," I began.

He put a finger on my lips. "If you tell your wish, it won't come true."

We made our silent wishes, and then Farrel took my face in his hands and gave me one more kiss, this one gentle.

"I'm wiped out," I said. "I don't know if I can make it home."

"I left you weak, huh?" He pulled me to him again.

Before we could kiss, Maylene and Justin slid into the front seat with us.

"Scoot over," Maylene ordered. "And honk again for Don and Frances."

A few minutes later, we saw Don tucking one side of his shirt in and Frances combing her hair with her fingers as they came moseying out of the woods toward the car.

"Hurry up!" Maylene yelled out the window

"They must have had to call timeout every two seconds to scratch mosquito bites," I said.

Farrel threw back his head and laughed. Everyone joined in, except Maylene.

"What's so funny?" Frances asked as she and Don got in back with Darcy and Larson.

"I wouldn't know," Maylene said, "You've made us late, and there's nothing at all funny about that."

Nobody said another word all the way back to the Dairyette, where we dropped the boys off at their cars. When Farrel slid out and I moved into the driver's seat, he whispered in my ear, "I'll call."

CHAPTER 17
There Is No Fire

Going into the house, I was practically bumping into walls with delirium, until I saw Mama waiting up in the den.

"Julia Lawrence Morgan, you're an hour late! What have you been doing?"

"Nothing."

"Nothing, the dog's foot. Go look at yourself in the mirror."

On the way to the bathroom, I racked my brains for what could be wrong. I had combed my hair and put on lipstick in the dark before coming inside. I flipped the bathroom light switch. Farrel's kissing had smeared my old lipstick from my chin to the bottom of my nose and up into my cheeks. The fresh lipstick made my lips stick out like bright-red neon in the center of a painted face.

I went back to the den, my face still red, but now from embarrassment as well as scrubbing.

"What do you have to say for yourself, young lady?" Mama asked.

"I'm in love."

"With whom?"

"Farrel."

"I told you I didn't want you going out with him."

"I didn't. I went out with the girls. We ran into the fellows."

"Where does he live?"

"On Baker."

"Oh God, I was afraid of that. Wrong side of the tracks."

"What matters is *who he is*, not how much money he comes from."

"I hope you never find out the truth about that. Remember, it's just as easy to fall in love with a rich man as a poor one."

"He's a boy, Mama, not a man."

"This is the one that comes home from college every weekend, isn't he?"

I nodded.

"When he should be staying at school and dating girls his own age. And where, pray tell, do you think he'll be able to get a job with a degree from Arkansas College?"

"We didn't talk about that," I said sarcastically.

"Or anything else, I suspect, from the way you look. Just how far did you go with this young man?"

"How far do you think with eight of us in the car?"

Mama visibly relaxed.

"He's only my first love, Mama. I might fall in love with a dozen more guys before I'm ready to get married."

"There is no fire like that of the first love," Mama said. "First loves have a strange way of staying in your heart forever." A look of profound sadness came over Mama's face. "Remember what Robert Frost said about his first love? Sixty years, and he still hadn't forgotten."

"But, Mama, I—"

"I just don't want you to be stuck with some ne'er-do-well in a trailer, living hand-to-mouth, and having a baby every year. You know very well what I'm driving at. Marry a man who'll support you."

I threw my hands in the air. "He's not even officially my boy-friend yet."

"And he didn't call you for the dance when he said he would," she said.

"Still, I think he likes me." A grin took over my face as I thought of his kisses. "And he might become my boyfriend, my *first* boyfriend. For once, I've got something all the other girls would give their eyeteeth for—a college guy to be in love with. Are you so old you can't understand anything?"

"Without a husband, I understand what it's like to be on the outside looking in," Mama said, world weary. "I don't want you to ever experience that."

"Having been a desperate and dateless Dilbert, I already have," I replied, getting up to leave the room.

"By the way." Her strange tone of voice stopped me. "I found this on your dresser. I'd like to know where you got it." She held up the picture of Carmen and me at the Valentine's dance.

"Eugene took it."

"I didn't ask you who took it. I asked where you got it."

"It's of me and my lookalike."

"That still doesn't answer my question. Did Eugene give it to you?"

"No, she did."

"She, being Carmen Whatever-her-name-is?"

"Newton. Carmen Newton. She handed it to me one day in the hall at school."

I crowded close to Mama's chair to look at the picture with her.

"I hate that we look so much alike, but in a way, it fascinates me. It's wild."

"The wildest," Mama said, barely articulating.

"You should see us together in the flesh. You won't believe it."

"The picture will suffice to give me the concept," Mama said. She was propping her feet on the straw-stuffed footstool, and once again, I was heading for my room, when the phone rang.

"It's after midnight. Who would be calling at this hour?" she said.

"I'll get it!"

I ran to the nearest phone extension in the breakfast room and sat on the ledge of one of the windows that opened into the den. Mama watched from her chair as I picked up the receiver.

"Hello," I said in my sexiest voice, certain that it was Farrel. It wasn't. My voice dropped into letdown mode. "Oh, hi."

"Who is it?" Mama asked.

"Did you get my valentine?" asked my father.

"Yes."

"Did you read the message inside?"

"Yes."

Mama sat forward in her chair. I put my hand over the mouthpiece. "It's *him!*" I said, rolling my eyes.

"Your father?" she mouthed back.

I nodded and held a finger to my lips.

"Tell him no," she hissed, getting up from her chair.

I forgot to whisper. "He hasn't said what he wants yet."

"He wants what he always wants," Mama said. "Trouble."

"I want you to set a date for a visit," my father said. "If you don't, you know what I'll do."

"I think I'd better go visit him," I whispered, my hand again over the mouthpiece.

"You know he gets violent when he drinks," Mama said with warning eyes as she moved close to me. "He's probably drunk now. Hang up."

"How about Saturday afternoon?" my father asked.

"I said, hang up!" Mama stepped closer and put her finger on the cutoff button of the phone.

"Mama!" I shrieked. "Now you've gone and done it!"

"He knows better than to call here at this hour. He must be blitzed out of his mind."

My hands shook. I wanted to go to my room, shut the door, and bawl. "He sounded sober."

Mama's face was taut. "Even if he's sober today, that's no guarantee he will be tomorrow. I don't want you exposed to that."

I didn't want to be exposed to it, either, but what choice did I have? I was scared to go on a visit with him—and scared not to. God knows, I didn't dare tell Mama what he had threatened on the phone the night of the bunking party.

CHAPTER 18
Dreams and Nightmares

April went by, and every time I saw her or talked on the phone with her, Maylene asked if Farrel had called yet. Every time she asked, I had to say, "No."

The week before finals, she slept over so we could study for the French exam. In the middle of conjugating the verb "aimer," our books and papers spread around us on my bed, I confessed.

"Maylene, *j'aime* Farrel."

She applauded. "You love Farrel? Wow! Now that's speaking French."

"He gives me a large charge."

"Why haven't you told me?"

"I was afraid you'd think I'm crazy to be in love with a boy who hasn't even asked me out."

"You are crazy. About him."

We fell over giggling.

"Guess who I'm crazy about," she said, sitting up. "Justin Moore. And he hasn't asked me out yet, either."

"Since when? The night we played Cockeye?"

"Before that. I just didn't say anything because of Steve, who I'm going to dump just as soon as Justin asks me out."

She reached for the bowl of popcorn sitting between us.

"You've been going with him for years."

"Yes, but everything Frances and the gang said about him is true. I tried to pretend it wasn't, but it is."

My eyes widened. "You mean you think he's—?"

She nodded. "He never kisses me, except sometimes at the door when he brings me home. And when he does, he comes at me with his lips puckered tight—like a cat's butt. And the last dance, when we passed that big mirror on the wall, he stopped dancing right in front of it and combed his hair."

I shook my head. "It's hard to believe. He's so good-looking."

"I talked it over with Daddy," she said. "He says Steve's *too* good-looking."

I stared at her. "You talked over something like that with your dad?"

"Oh, yes. I depend on Daddy. Mother would have died if I'd brought up something like that with her."

"So would Mama," I said.

Her face reddened. "Oops, I forgot about your dad, Julie. Look, maybe it's none of my business, but we're such good friends now, I feel I can ask. You see your dad, don't you?"

I studied the bluebird pattern on my bedspread.

"Only when I absolutely have to."

"Could you ever talk over something like this with him?"

I couldn't repress a sarcastic laugh. "He and I don't talk, Maylene."

"It must be awful, not having your dad around."

Intending to sound flip, I said, "Not at all." What came out was a shrill tone that made me cringe.

She looked back down at her notebook.

"We don't have to talk about this, if it gets you upset."

"I'm not upset!" I took a deep breath and tried keep my voice steady. "The truth is, sometimes he scares me."

She looked at me in disbelief. "He scares you?"

"Whisper. Mama would have a conniption fit if she heard me talking to you about him." I took a breath. "When she divorced him, the lawyers she works for now pulled some strings and kept him from having any rights to visit me for a long time. It didn't seem to bother him until I was four. Then, one night . . ."

"I've got cold chills already," Maylene said, rubbing her upper arms.

I could feel my heart doing the speedo routine it always did when I thought back on that night.

"He came here. Mama saw him park and get out of the car. She snatched me up and hid me in the closet."

"Oh, my gosh," Maylene's hands flew to her cheeks.

"He pounded on the door with his fists, and then Mama cried out, 'He's got an iron pipe!'"

"An iron pipe?"

I waved one hand frantically. "Quiet."

Her face splotched. "Sorry."

"I opened the closet door a crack and saw his face through the glass in the front door. It was all twisted—in a snarl. He raised the iron pipe and smashed the glass in the door."

"You must've been scared to death."

"Mama called the police, and they came sirening out. When they got up onto the porch, I ran out of the closet and hung onto Mama's skirt. The neighbors on both sides were gathered on our lawn, watching. I nearly die of embarrassment when I think about it. We were a spectacle. For years, I hid my face whenever I saw any of them. I feel like hiding it now."

She patted my hand.

"Maylene, have you ever heard anyone gossiping about it?"

She hesitated a long moment, then finally said, "My folks only told me he'd been arrested. So, clue me. What on earth happened next?"

I entwined my fingers and ordered myself to stop trembling.

"While the police were handcuffing him, he mouthed to me, 'I love you.' Can you believe it? What a stupid thing for him to do! He'd only ever seen me from a distance. How could he love me?"

"You're his daughter. Naturally, he would love you."

"He was my father, and I didn't love him."

"He still is . . . your father."

"And I still don't!"

"How can you say that?"

"Because I don't. Not one small bit. He means nothing to me. I can't think of him as a father."

"But, you said you do see him?"

"When he got out of jail, the courts gave him visitation rights, so I have to, once in a while, but I hate it. Half the time he's bombed out of his mind." I pressed on my stomach to get a deep breath. "Every time I saw him, Mama had to take me to the court house to turn me over to him so she could have police protection."

Maylene peered into my face with anxious eyes.

"Do the police go with you on the visit?"

I shook my head.

"If he's that dangerous, why would she let you go with him?"

"Yeah, really. I've never understood that."

We sat in silence for several minutes.

"It was a court order, so I guess she has no choice," I said, finally. "So far, he never has done anything—to hurt me, I mean. He sometimes brings me a present when I see him. I never want to visit him again."

"Why?"

"He's always drunk when I go, and I'm scared he'll get violent. I hate it!"

"Can you get away with not going?" Maylene asked.

"I don't know. He threatened me."

"When?"

"The night Elvis sang on TV and we had the bunking party. Remember, the phone rang?"

"And you wouldn't say who had called."

"It was Big Daddy. He said, if I didn't visit him, he was going to go to court and have his fishing buddy, Judge Hammond, enforce his visitation rights."

"Oh, my God. What if he does?"

A night breeze blew the frothy curtains at my windows.

"The worst thing would be if he won a custody suit to take me away from Mama. That's her biggest nightmare."

"Aren't you too old to be fought over like that?" Maylene asked. "I would think, at fifteen, you'd have some say-so in the matter."

"It's eighteen."

"Those lawyers your mother works for, she could ask them for help."

I glanced over my shoulder toward the door.

"Mama absolutely can't find out about his threat."

Maylene looked thoughtful. "So, what are you going to do?"

"Stall, for as long as I can." I chewed the end of my pencil.

"Why don't you head him off? Go for a visit with him. Since he's never done anything to harm you, would one visit be so bad? Take the car, and if he gets violent, leave."

"I guess I *ought* to visit him, but I don't want to. And maybe I *ought* to love him, but I don't."

Maylene shook her head ever so slightly and looked away.

A week later, I was at the Rialto Theatre downtown with the gang, watching Ingrid Bergman in *Anastasia*, when I heard the sound of rustling crinoline in the aisle. Someone stooped down next to my end seat and propped her elbows on the chair arm. It was Carmen.

"I have to tell you something," she said.

Heads on all sides turned in our direction.

"Right now?" I hissed.

"Yes, right now. My mother told me—we're kin to each other."

"Keep it down, will ya?" a voice said.

"We can't talk here," Carmen whispered, and the rustling sound of her skirt receded back up the aisle.

I waited a few minutes, then followed her.

CHAPTER 19
CONFUSION

I threw myself against the theatre door and rushed outside. The night heat swamped me. I looked all around. No sight of Carmen or the old car.

But Farrel was there, stretching one long leg out of a dark-blue Chrysler Imperial a half block up the street on Cedar. His dishwater-blond hair shone in the mellow haze of streetlights as he moved around the back of the car—and saw me.

"Julie!" He flashed a smile. "I came looking for you, but I didn't expect to find you outside. Isn't the movie any good?"

"It's good. I'm just—rattled. Someone said something that blew me out of my tree."

His brows furrowed as he looked down at me. "Who? I'll knock his block off." He took my hands and held them against his pale-blue shirt.

"It wasn't a he. Remember the girl who looks like me?"

Farrel cocked his head. "Ah."

"She told me we're kin."

He studied my anxious eyes. "What's so bad about that? Everyone in Union County is kin to each other."

"The crowd doesn't want her running with us. If we're kin, she'll want to tag along with me everywhere."

I sensed that he wanted me to simmer down. "How did you know I was here?"

"Your mother." He shrugged. "I think I flubbed the dub."

"What happened?"

"I called to see if you wanted to go out for a coke—or something."
He gave me a knowing look. "Your mother said it was way too late to
be calling you to go somewhere tonight. I think she would've jerked a
knot in me, if I'd been in reach."

Silently, I counted to ten.

"Mama's old-fashioned. She thinks a date should be made at least a
week in advance."

Farrel loosened his fingers from mine.

"I don't know what I'm going to be doing one *day* to the next, never
mind a week. Guess that does me in with her."

I grasped his fingers back. "Just ignore her. I like doing things on the
spur of the moment."

"In that case, my old man's car is right there." He pointed toward the
blue Chrysler Imperial. "Let's go."

"I brought Maylene and the crowd in Mama's car. I can't leave them."

"Give the keys to Maylene. She can drive the others home. We'll go
by her house later to pick up your car."

The theatre door flew open. "Julie!" Maylene rushed out. "What on
earth is going on? Where *is* that girl?" Seeing Farrel, she stopped short
and turned on her heavy drawl. "Oh hi, Farrel."

"She's gone." I turned wide eyes on Maylene, signaling her to can
it. "Farrel wants me to go somewhere with him. If you'll drive the
others home in my car, he'll take me to your house later to pick it up."
I dangled the car keys in front of her.

She frowned. "You know I can't do that."

"But why?"

"Insurance. What if I had a wreck or something?"

"You won't have a wreck." I pleaded with my face.

"I just can't be responsible for your mother's car. You understand,
don't you, Farrel?"

He mumbled something unintelligible.

Maylene's face lit up, and she snapped her fingers. "I've got it! Why
don't we leave your car here and *all* go with Farrel to the Dairyette?"

I waited for Farrel to tell her we planned to go alone, but he didn't. He did look taken aback, but he said nothing.

Maylene batted her eyelashes at him. "Is that all right with you, Farrel?"

His pained expression revealed that this whole scene had mushroomed into something he didn't want to be involved in.

When he didn't answer, she said, "Great. I'll get Frances and Darcy. The movie is over. They're inside, yakking. We'll just be a minute."

"Maylene!" I rushed back inside the theatre after her and shut the door. "What are you doing? Farrel wanted to be *alone* with me."

"He didn't say that."

"He said it to me!"

"I know you certainly want to be alone with him, but, Julie, he won't have any respect for you if you go prancing off with him when he hasn't even called."

"He did call! Tonight! He told me so. Only I wasn't home. Please, take my car. You know how much I want to go out with him."

"You'll end up going parking, right?"

Warmth rushed over me at the thought of Farrel's kisses.

Maylene turned into Mama.

"That's the plan. I can see it on your face. If you're not careful, he'll think you're easy—that he doesn't even have to buy you a coke to get you to put out, never mind take you on a *real* date."

"I'm *not* putting out! I don't understand you, Maylene. You want me to have a cute boy to date, and when I'm about to get one, you throw a wrench in the works."

"I'm just saying, you need to play a little hard to get. Otherwise, you'll come across looking like that Carmen creature. You know we don't want anyone like that running with us." She looked toward the theatre doors. "Where did she go, anyway?"

"I don't know."

"I heard her say you all are kin."

"Everybody in the whole theatre heard. Go on, go with Farrel. I'm going home. The night's ruined for me, anyway."

I stormed back out the door, nearly crashing headlong into Farrel, who stood restlessly, jangling his car keys.

"What's the story?" he asked.

"Maylene won't do it. They're all going with you," I said, swallowing hard. "I'm going home. I wouldn't be very good company, anyway. I don't like being part of a harem."

He reached out and tucked a wisp of my hair behind my ear.

"I'll give you a call, when I can plan far enough ahead, and we'll go out, just the two of us. Okay?"

I nodded, and he lightly kissed my lips.

Up the street, I looked back at his car. The girls were piling in. Maylene crawled into the front seat next to him.

Insurance my eye!

CHAPTER 20
A Deal with Mama

Mama was in her nightgown, asleep in her easy chair—the TV blaring—when I burst in through the back door.

She startled awake, one breast slipping partially out of the low-cut, lacy V of her gown.

"You're home." She pulled the strap back up on her shoulder. "It's only nine thirty."

"I know."

"Is something wrong?"

"I can't believe what you said to Farrel Budrow when he called here tonight."

"Turn off the dope machine so I can stay awake."

"Why were you so rude to him?" I asked on the way to switch off the TV.

She took a sip of tea from the sweating glass on the end table.

"Honey, my ice is melted. Get me some more, and we'll talk about it."

In the kitchen, I slung a few cubes into her glass.

"Don't forget to refill the ice tray," she called.

Back in the den, I thrust the glass at her so hard that tea sloshed onto her nightie.

"We'll have no tantrums, young lady," she said, "not even wordless."

"I've waited weeks for Farrel to call me."

"If he were interested, he'd have called long before this."

"He's interested, all right. He came to the Rialto looking for me."
Mama's eyebrow shot up. "And?"

I sat on one of the red couches. "I couldn't go with him because I had the car, and Maylene wouldn't take it and drive the others home."

Mama slapped her thigh. "Good for Maylene. At least one of you young'uns has some sense." She lowered her voice. "He isn't worthy of you, honey."

"You say that about everybody, except Eugene Hoffmeyer. You don't even know a thing about Farrel's folks. You just don't approve of where they live. His father drives a big, gorgeous Chrysler Imperial, I'll have you know."

"Some people spend all their money on showy cars when they don't have a pot to pee in. When the time comes, I want you to marry someone who will take care of you, not a bum like . . ." She twisted the small garnet ring on her pinky.

"My father?"

"Yes."

"I knew when I married him our upbringing was different, but I ignored that little fact, thinking I could change him. Your father and I had different values, and so do you and Mr. Budrow."

I jumped to my feet. "You've never even met him!"

"I don't have to. He's demonstrated that he is not a man of his word."

"How?"

"He doesn't do what he says he'll do. Have you forgotten the Valentine dance so soon?"

"Only that one time, and we had just met."

Under Mama's cynical stare, I sank back down on one of the red couches. I didn't want her to be right, but I knew she probably was.

After a few moments of uncomfortable silence, I said, "Something else happened tonight. That Carmen girl came up to me during the movie and told me her mother said we're kin."

Mama clucked her tongue. "Don't forget, you had a marrying great-grandpa. Married four times. He probably had a little fun on the other side of the blanket, too." She took a sip of her tea. "Umm, not enough sugar now. Nothing is ever as good as the first glass."

"I don't want to be kin to her. The crowd doesn't like her."

Mama tilted her head. "It occurs to me that she wants to use you as her ticket in with the popular kids. I think you should ignore her."

"How do you propose I do that when I see her every day at school? Maylene and the others heard her, too. You think they're going to forget?"

Mama got up and crossed to the back door and locked it.

"They'll forget because it isn't about them. Leave it alone, and it'll blow over in a day or so. I guarantee you."

"I feel like she's turning into me, somehow."

"That's ridiculous."

"No, it isn't. Having her around is like losing what makes me, *me*. My uniqueness."

Mama looked thoughtful. "Perhaps I should send you to Harriman School for Girls in Dallas."

My jaw dropped. "What?"

"It's a very exclusive girls' school. Come to think of it, that's exactly what you need. It would get you away from her and far enough away from your father that he'd leave us alone."

"I don't want to go there."

"I'll telephone the school on Monday." Mama got up and headed for the kitchen with her glass. "I'm going to start all over with this iced tea."

"I won't go! You can't make me!" I called after her.

Mama turned and stood tall, like a general. "You're my daughter. You'll do as I say."

"Mama, what is this?" I pleaded, changing my tone. "Are you trying to get rid of me?"

Her eyes filled with a spiritual light. "I want to provide the finer things in life for you, and I want you to be happy."

"I wouldn't be happy at a girls' school. If you try to send me there, I'll do more than visit my father. I'll go *live* with him."

Mama laid the back of one hand against her forehead and launched into her martyr act.

"How could you threaten me with such a thing?"

"It's called retaliation. You're threatening *me*."

"You know my biggest fear is that by dent and maneuver he'll win custody of you." She came to the couch and hugged me close. "You know I'm not trying to get rid of you." Pulling back, she looked into my face with anxious eyes. "I just don't want you to be hurt."

I fought the tears slipping out of my eyes.

"Hush now," Mama said, pulling me close again and rubbing my back. "You don't have to go away to school, provided you do as I say."

"About what?" I asked, pulling away from her.

She took hold of my shoulders and looked into my eyes. "Forget about that girl. Don't go trying to investigate and ferret out information that has no truth to it. Have nothing to do with her. Will you promise me that?"

I looked at her for a long moment.

"I'll make a deal with you."

"I'm your mother. I don't make deals for good behavior."

"You will, if you want my promise."

"You've gotten awful sassy lately," she said.

I gave her a defiant stare.

"All right. What is it you want?"

"Give Farrel another chance. And say he doesn't have to call a week in advance for me to go out with him."

Mama went back to her chair, crossed her legs, and touched the tips of her fingers together, like a doctor about to prescribe a cure.

"Very well, then. You may go out with him, *if* he calls at least a day in advance. But I'm afraid that's a mighty big if."

CHAPTER 21
O Happy Day

Farrel did call again—but not until school had been out for four long weeks. On the day before my birthday, the phone rang just as Mama was about to leave for work. I skidded into the side of her bed, rushing to get it.

"Hello."

"Who is it?" Mama mouthed.

"Oh hi, Farrel," I gave Mama a smug smile.

When we hung up, I sashayed past her on the way to my room.

"He called."

"I noticed," she said.

"A day ahead, so we're going out at seven thirty tomorrow night. Happy Birthday to me!"

She trailed after me and lingered in the doorway.

"I was planning on fixing you a nice birthday dinner and taking us to the show. I've already bought the groceries."

"You can still fix a nice dinner," I said, ignoring the face she put on to make me feel guilty. "But early, so I can be ready when he comes."

"How does Farrel spell his last name?" Mama asked, her voice disdainful.

"B-u-d-r-o-w. Why?"

"It sounds French, but an upper class family would spell it B-o-u-d-r-e-a-u. At any rate, it sounds foreign."

"If it is, that would be great, since we're foreign."

She blinked. "What are you talking about?"

"The blood royal from the Murphys, remember? Kings of Ireland?" I pinched her cheek. "I should think that makes us foreign."

Mama scowled. "You're incorrigible."

"You said it, not me. Anyway, Farrel's American, just like you and me. I don't know what kind of a name Budrow is, but I love it. Someday, I just might be Mrs. Budrow. That makes me want to dance through the house singing."

"This will probably help you."

I tore into the flat package she handed me.

"It's from Elvis! Oh look, a new forty-five. 'I Want You, I Need You, I Love You.' What a title! I can't wait to hear it."

"I have to leave in two minutes," Mama said, straightening the collar of her short-sleeved, navy suit coat. "Hurry up. Read me his note."

"If I don't, are you going to tear up my room looking for it?"

Mama drew herself up tall. "I've never read any of your letters."

I gave her a withering glare.

Looking off to the side with guilty eyes, she added, "Except those you've left out in plain view."

"Underneath the mattress of my bed is *not* plain view."

Her lips twitched with a repressed smile.

"Mama, you are so bad."

She tweaked me under the chin. "Come on now, give your old Mama something interesting to think about while she's wearing her fingers to the bone pounding away at that typewriter all day."

I sighed. "Okay, I give."

Dear Juliet,
I appeared on the Milton Berle show early this month. Did you happen to catch it?

"How did we miss that?" I cried.

I sang a new song, "Hound Dog," which has really stirred up a ruckus. They've started calling me "Elvis the Pelvis." I don't like them calling me

*that, but the worst thing they're saying is I'm going to destroy you kids'
morals. It makes me sick, but there's nothing I can do about it. The song is
what it is, and I'm committed to it. Steve Allen is going to make me wear
a tuxedo when I sing it on his show the first of July, and get this, I have to
sing it to a real, live hound dog. That's gonna look so stupid.*

*Anyway, I'm sending another song I think you'll like, and I'll send you
"Hound Dog" as soon as we record it. Gotta run for now. My fried peanut
butter and banana sandwich is getting cold. You be good, you hear? And
don't forget—I'll remember you.*
Elvis

"Fried peanut butter and banana sandwich," Mama exclaimed. "The
very idea makes me nauseous."

"It couldn't be anywhere near as bad as salt mackerel."

Mama gazed past me.

"*The Steve Allen Show*. He *is* moving up." Then she smiled and gave
me a peck on the check. "I must dash. The lawyers are finishing briefs
today. I'll, no doubt, be late getting home. Will you open a can of
something for supper?"

"What?"

"How about Vienna Sausages and sauerkraut?"

"Double urp slop!"

After she left, I put on the new record and dialed Maylene.

"Guess what, guess what, guess what! Farrel called me for a date! O
happy day!"

"It's about time."

"That's not all. Elvis sent a new record!"

"All in one morning? You must be over the moon. Justin asked me
for a date to the TAC House dance tonight. Why don't you and Farrel
sit next to us?"

Happiness whizzed out of me like air blasting out of a balloon.

"My date with Farrel is for tomorrow night."

"Oooh nooo!" she exclaimed. "Do you suppose he's taking someone
else to the dance?"

"He probably isn't even going," I said.

"I wouldn't count on that. Farrel shows up at all the dances." There was a moment of silence. "Well, at least he finally asked you for a date. Do you have a date to the dance tonight?"

"No."

"Aww, that's too bad." More silence. "I thought you were calling to tell me what you plan on doing about Carmen and her tale that you all are kin."

"I'm planning on doing nothing."

"Nothing?" Maylene gasped. "I'm horrified. You have to do something. She's spreading it all over town."

"School's out. There's not much spreading she can do now."

"Justin told me she was spreading it all around at the Youth Fellowship supper just last Sunday."

"Oh no!"

"You don't want to be kin to a girl like that."

I tried to gather my thoughts.

"Actually, we don't even know her."

"We know she's cheap. We can tell that by the way she dresses. That says it all, if you ask me."

I said nothing.

"You want to run around with us, don't you?" she pressed.

"You know I do," I answered, meekly. "You're my best friend."

"All right, then."

I twisted the phone cord.

"Maylene, I promised Mama I'd leave it alone. If I don't, she's going to send me to Dallas to a girls' school."

"A girls' school? That would be death before dying. She wouldn't really do it, would she?"

"You don't know Mama. She will."

"Still, you have to do something," Maylene said. "Wait a minute while I think."

My ear felt like a smashed cauliflower against the receiver.

"I know!" she finally exclaimed. "We could just casually drop in at Woolworths for lunch."

"I don't get it."

"Carmen works there. Surely you knew that."

I could barely speak. "No, I didn't."

"Well, get this. While Mother and I were downtown yesterday getting me a dress for the dance, we had lunch at Woolworths, and Carmen served us. Oh, and guess what else?"

More bad news?

"I finally got down to a hundred and ten pounds."

I could just see her gloating face. For a month, we'd been racing to lose down from a hundred and twenty to a hundred and ten.

"What do you weigh these days?" she asked, her singsong drawl grating in my ear.

"One fourteen, and I don't care. I'm gonna have a fried peanut butter and banana sandwich for lunch. That's one of Elvis's favorite foods. So there. Farrel obviously likes me like I am."

She tittered. "If you say so."

I ignored her.

"Still, you should try the Hugh Goodwin School P.T.A.'s new Soda Fountain Diet. It was in the newspaper. One of the lunches is a tuna fish sandwich on toast, with ice cream for dessert."

"That doesn't sound like a reducing diet."

"Listen girl, don't knock it. The Soda Fountain Diet works. Anyway, I asked Carmen if she was making friends and getting adjusted."

"That sounds like you're planning on being her friend."

"Heavens, no. I just wanted to see what I could find out. Boy, did I get an earful."

"Tell, tell!"

"Guess who she thinks is the cutest boy in El Dorado? None other than Farrel Budrow."

My stomach sank to the bedsprings.

"He hasn't taken her out, has he?"

"I wouldn't be surprised, the way she was talking about him."

I tingled with unpleasant shock. "What did she say?"

"Oh, nothing really. Just that he's cute and all. Listen, forget about peanut butter and bananas. That's sure to push you right back up to a hundred and twenty. Let's go for tuna fish and ice cream at Woolworths.

We'll get there early, before the lunch crowd, and she might have a minute to chat. You can get both stories right from the horse's mouth—whether she's been out with Farrel and how you all are kin."

"But I promised Mama I wouldn't."

"You didn't promise not to go out to lunch with me. You can't help it if you *happen* to run into Carmen. Come on, Julie, go with me. Please."

I never would have dreamed in a million years that Maylene McCord would beg me to go to lunch with her.

"You might even lose a pound before your date with Farrel tomorrow."

That sealed it.

"Okay, but if anyone sees us . . ."

"No one will. I'll pick you up at eleven fifteen. Be ready. We're going to get to the bottom of this Carmen mystery."

CHAPTER 22
The Lunch Counter at Woolworths

"I'll become a prisoner in girls' school, if Mama finds out about this," I said as Maylene and I approached the door to Woolworths.

"She won't. We'll be in disguise." She handed me a red polka-dotted headscarf. "Tie that on, and wear your sunglasses. I heard that crazy people think no one can see them if they have on their sunglasses. Maybe it'll work for us."

"Maybe so," I said, "since we're both crazy to be doing this."

Inside, we darted behind a rack of housedresses and peeped out to case the lunch counter.

"Do you see anyone we know?" I whispered.

"Do I see Carmen is the question," Maylene said. "And yes, I do. Behind the counter."

My stomach rolled. "Maybe this isn't such a good idea."

"Come on." Maylene tugged my arm. "We've come this far. The rest'll be a piece of cake."

"You don't mean this diet lets us have cake?"

"Only on Fridays." She grinned. "But today's Friday."

At the counter, Carmen stood pouring a glass of iced tea for a white-haired man. He turned to glance at us.

"Oh God, it's Judge Hammond," I said to Maylene as we slipped onto the red, plastic-covered stools a few seats down. "He's the judge who granted my father visitation rights."

"Hello, Julie," he said, beaming.

I managed a sick smile back at him and snatched a menu from between the salt and pepper shakers and the sugar cylinder.

"So much for our wonderful disguises," I mouthed to Maylene.

With elbows propped on the black marble counter and one hand masking my face on the judge's side, I pretended to study the specials.

Judge Hammond flagged Carmen down as she approached us with her order pad.

"Box me up a piece of cherry pie to go, honey," he said and, pulling out his wallet, he tossed a five dollar bill on the counter.

"Keep the change," he said to Carmen when she returned with the pie. "Say hello to your father for me, Julie."

"Judas Priest," I whispered and watched him propel his stubby bulk out the front door.

"Hi, Carmen," Maylene drawled, sounding super friendly. "How are you?"

"Peachy."

When I glanced up at her, she smiled a satisfied smile.

"Come to get the low down on what I told you?"

"We came to have lunch, not discuss your fantasy life," I answered, my voice tight.

She put one hand on her hip. "Well, excuse me. What'll ya have?"

"Tuna fish salad on toast and peach ice cream with chocolate cake for dessert," Maylene chirped.

"The same for me," I said, staring hard at the menu. "And iced tea."

"Me, too. Tea," Maylene said.

"So you want to know how we're kin?" Carmen asked.

"You're probably the result of my marrying great-grandpa," I said. "I don't think I care to know which side of the blanket you came from."

Carmen laughed. "You'd rather discuss your fantasy life, huh?" Striding away, she spouted our order, way too loud, to the cook, who stood scowling at us.

"What's the matter with you?" Maylene hissed. "We came here to get to the bottom of this. Now you've ticked her off."

"I'm just freaked, that's all."

Two people came to the counter and sat on the stools next to me. Thankfully, I didn't know them. When Carmen finished taking their orders, I crooked a finger at her.

"Okay," I said in a low voice. "Say what you have to say."

"I'm busy now." With a smug look, she walked away.

Maylene moved two stools farther down the counter and motioned to me.

"Scoot down here, and don't have a cow, no matter what she says."

At that moment, I saw a familiar face, sashaying past fabrics and notions, just one counter over from where we sat. My pulse jolted, and I ducked under the counter.

"What the matter?" Maylene asked, her upside-down face peering at me.

"It's Mavis MacAfee. Mama's best friend."

I could hear Carmen slap our drinks onto the counter. She called out, "Want yours down there?"

"Get up, Julie," ordered Maylene. "Mavis's on her way to the checkout counter up front. She'll never spot you."

I climbed back up on my stool and fanned my face with a menu.

Maylene, ever the would-be lady, said "Thank you" to Carmen.

"De nada," Carmen replied, looking at me. "Okay, I've got a sec."

"How do you know Farrel Budrow?" I blurted.

She blinked. "Whoa, that's out of the blue."

I said nothing.

She shrugged. "He comes in here for coffee some days. We shoot the breeze. What's it to you, anyway?"

"I just wondered."

"Do you go with him or just have hot pants for him?" Carmen quipped.

Maylene clipped her charm-school smile.

I bristled.

"So it's hot pants, huh?" Carmen said with a laugh.

"We have a date for tomorrow night," I said, sounding too la-di-da.

"Sounds like it's your first. Oops, gotta serve up an order."

"She may be trashy, but she's also smart," Maylene said with a nod. "She must speak fluent Italian."

"De nada is Spanish," I said, "and I bet she doesn't know another word."

"Isn't this fun?" Maylene said with a giggle, but I could barely smile. The atmosphere was as taut as the elastic in a garter belt.

"Since you don't go with Farrel Budrow, what is between you?" Carmen asked when she came back with our food. "Are you so snowed you just let him take you to the woods and feel you up?"

I spewed a mouthful of tea all over Carmen's white uniform. Another cough erupted from the person sitting next to me.

"Cool it, girlie. I gotta wear this all day," Carmen said with a little smirk. "Guess I hit the nail on the head about that." She glanced over her shoulder at the scowling cook. "I need to get back to work. We can't talk here, anyway. If you'll come to my house at six fourteen East Third this afternoon at five thirty, I'll give you the whole enchilada about us being kin. I've been wanting to get together with you, anyway." She threw a glance at Maylene. "And all you gals."

With that, she left Maylene and me staring at our soggy tuna sandwiches.

"We didn't get very far with this," Maylene said, "but she isn't dating Farrel." She gave my arm a friendly nudge. "At least you found out that much."

"Mama's right," I mused. "She's just trying to break into our crowd. There's no way I'm going over to her house."

CHAPTER 23
Old Spice and the Drive-In

Farrel's knock was soft the next evening. I flipped out at the sight of him, smiling at me beneath the porch light. His blue, short-sleeved shirt and dark slacks gave his lanky frame a casual, appealing look. The scene burned itself into my memory. Our first date on my birthday. It was a perfect gift from the universe, in spite of my secret embarrassment at the night bugs bobbing around his head. I raged inside that my family was so screwed up there still was no yellow bug light.

"This is Farrel," I said to Mama, who had come to the door to meet him.

"It's nice to meet you, Mrs. Morgan."

Wow! That sounded like a gentleman raised on Country Club Lane, instead of a poor boy from the wrong side of the tracks.

Knowing very well he wasn't, Mama asked, in her pretentious society voice, "Your last name is French, is it not?"

"Yes, ma'am."

"And you spell it . . . ?"

Farrel fixed his eyes on the wrinkle between Mama's brows.

"Like below the salt folks, not the upper crust."

Mama put on an "I knew I was right" smile.

A beat later, Farrel gave my upper arm a make-believe punch.

"Hey, Julie, is it true you're Elvis Presley's girlfriend?"

Weird though it was, Mama bridled with pride.

"He sends her all his new records. The house rocks and rolls day and night."

"Elvis and I are just friends, and long distance ones, at that." I tugged gently on Farrel's arm. "See you later, Mama."

But Farrel lingered.

"I'm taking her to the drive-in, if that's all right with you, Mrs. Morgan."

Mama's eyes brightened. "That'll be fine. I'm pleased you asked. I don't expect that from most young folks these days. Don't get it, either. But don't think you can cotton up to me and get away with anything."

He laughed. "No, ma'am. What time should I have her home?"

"Eleven o'clock," Mama said without missing a beat.

"It's Saturday night. Can't I at least stay out till twelve?"

She looked first at him, then at me.

"Well, since it's your birthday, okay, but if you aren't home on the dot, I'll send out a posse. And you know I can."

"Thanks, Mama."

I gave her a kiss and started out onto the porch, but her next words stopped me.

"Judge Hammond said the tuna sandwiches were good at Woolworths yesterday."

I looked quickly at her.

"And Mavis said she liked the head scarf you were wearing."

I thought my eyes would roll clear up into my head. Caught, in polka-dotted red. I teetered at her next words, and Farrel caught my arm.

"I'm delighted that you and Maylene had lunch together."

"What was all that about?" he asked on the way to the dark-blue Chrysler sitting in the driveway.

"She found out I ate at Woolworths, but she's not mad, so she didn't find out why. If she had, I'd be on my way to a girls' school."

He opened the door for me and waved to Mama, still watching us at the door, as he went around the front of the car to get in.

"Why did you go there?"

"To talk to Carmen."

"What about? How y'all are kin?"

"Yes." *And whether she's been out with you.*

"So, how are you?"

"I don't think we are. Mama thinks Carmen just wants to break into our crowd and made me promise not to have anything to do with her."

He stretched an arm across the wide car seat and pulled me over next to him.

"You better be good and mind your Mama. We don't want you shipped off. But don't be too good." He laughed low. "Speaking of good, you sure do smell good."

"So do you," I said. "What is that scent?"

"Old Spice."

"It sends me."

He burst into the first few bars of the popular song, "You Send Me," then broke off, laughing.

"Tell that Elvis fellow to move over."

The streetlights glowed in the summer night as we drove through our little town. Without thinking, I spouted, "'O, she doth teach the torches to burn bright!'"

He gave me a look. "Say what?"

"It's a line from a Shakespeare play we read in English class," I said. "*Romeo and Juliet.*"

He turned an amazed face toward me.

"Oh yes, old Willie boy. Not my bag. But that's cool, you being able to quote that highbrow stuff. Hardly anybody can understand that kind of talk, anymore."

"Our teacher read it aloud to us. She made it all so clear."

We drove along in silence while I fretted that the Shakespeare business had turned him off.

He squeezed my knee. "So how old are you today, birthday girl?"

"Sixteen."

He winked at me. "I'll give you a present, when we get to the drive-in."

"How can you? You didn't even know it was my birthday."

"The best presents are those you make yourself. Isn't that what they say? Hey, I looked for you at the dance last night."

"You went to the dance?"

"Oh, yeah. You sound surprised. I always like to stop in at the dances. I didn't see you, so I had to dance with Maylene."

Maylene hadn't said a word about seeing Farrel or dancing with him.

"I'd have asked you to go, but I figured it was too late for a dance by your Mama's standards."

"What movie are we going to?" I asked, eager to change the subject.

"What difference does it make?" His laugh was low and sexy.

I half laughed along with him, but I didn't know what was funny.

At the drive-in, he hooked the speaker over the car window. Then he opened the glove compartment and took out a box containing a coiled, green thing.

"Hold this a minute while I find the matches."

I took it between two fingers and held it at arm's length. "What is it?"

He looked surprised. "PIC. You light it, and the smoke keeps away mosquitoes. You must not go to the drive-in much."

"A few times. Last week, Darcy drove the Dreamsicle, and eight of us squeezed into the trunk and sneaked in, while she and Maylene only bought two tickets."

"Hey, that's cool."

"The ticket booth boy let us get all the way to a parking place before he came running up and caught us half in and half out of the trunk."

He struck a match and lit the PIC. An odor, like incense, spread throughout the car.

"Serves you right. Anyway, this stuff'll keep you from going home with bites all over you." Again, his laugh was low and sexy. "Unless they're my love bites."

I heard the beginning of the Twentieth Century Fox music blare out of the speaker, but I only saw a few minutes of the movie. Farrel laid one long, deep kiss after another on me. The smell of Old Spice mingling with his faint scent of perspiration made me feel faint. I couldn't resist his kisses. Didn't want to. Didn't try.

In the middle of one, his hand brushed my breast. A few minutes later, it happened again, only this time the hand lingered.

"Don't, Farrel." But he didn't stop—probably because I moaned when I said it. "Farrel, you . . . we aren't supposed to do that."

"It won't hurt for a boy to mash you, Julie," he mumbled, drawing me down lower onto the seat behind the steering wheel.

So Farrel was what Mama called a masher.

Scared that if I *didn't* let him, I'd lose him before I even had him, I gave in and stopped pushing his hand away. The next minute, he was undoing the top button of my blouse.

"No!" I cried, struggling to sit up. "We can't."

"Julie, you're so beautiful, and you feel so good."

How could a girl resist that kind of talk? I swallowed as he undid the next button and slipped his hand inside. By the middle of the kiss, his fingers were inside my *bra*. This could *not* happen!

"Farrel, you have to stop!" I cried, pushing him away and sitting up.

"I thought you wanted me to." He stared, glassy-eyed, through the windshield at the movie screen, while I fumbled to rebutton. "Come on, Julie," he said, "all the college girls I know will let a boy put his hand in there and play."

"I'm not in college," I said.

"Frances lets Don. I know that for a fact," he said.

"I don't want to get a bad reputation."

"You won't. I never kiss and tell."

"Obviously, Don does."

"Well, I don't." He crossed his heart with his middle finger.

"That's the finger you use to flip the bird," I said.

He gave me a sideways frown. "You're not one of them complicated girls, are you?"

His bad grammar brought home Mama's sermons about not dating boys from the wrong side of the tracks.

"I'm not complicated, but I do know that boys don't respect girls who let them . . . do that."

A whine hummed in my ear.

"Mosquitoes!" he exclaimed, stretching to scratch his ankle. "That PIC must not be working. Let's blow this place."

I was still checking buttons when we got to the Dairyette. We got a coke, then Farrel asked, "What time is it?"

"My watch says ten o' five."

"We've got time."

"Time for what?"

"I know a place I want to take you. Another part of your birthday present. You'll love it."

And I did. It was about three miles from our house, not far off Highway 82 that went to Magnolia. We parked near a bushy tree, silhouetted in the moonlight.

Farrel turned up the radio and got out, pulling me gently past the steering wheel.

"Come on."

"What is that sweet smell?" I asked.

"An old plum tree. The plums must be ripe. It don't belong to nobody. We can pick all we want."

"It must belong to someone."

"Julie, Julie, you worry too much."

He picked a plum and took a bite. "Hmmm, so good. Here."

He held it out to me. The juicy flesh of the plum was sweet.

While the summer moon floated in and out of wispy clouds above us, we filled our hands with the juicy plums.

"We should wish on a star," he said.

"The moon is so bright, you can't see any stars," I said. From the car radio, The Platters' "Only You" filled the night. "Can't we wish without a star?"

He shook his head. "It wouldn't be the same."

He went to the trunk of the car and came back with a paper bag and an old blanket, which he spread on the ground.

"Here." He handed me the bag. "Put the plums in this, and take 'em home to your mother."

"You'd better take them home to *your* mother," I said with a sardonic laugh.

"Julie," he whispered.

He reached for me. I flung my plums over his shoulder and threw my arms around him. His lips found mine. Elvis's "I Want You, I Need You, I Love You" radiated out into the night. We sank to the blanket in a deep kiss. A minute later, he fumbled with my buttons again. I stiffened.

"It feels good, don't it?" he asked, his tone soothing.

"Well . . ."

"Tell the truth," he said.

"Well, yes, but . . ."

"And you want *me* to do it to you, don't you?"

"I don't want you to think I'm cheap or loose. I want you to respect me."

He turned earnest eyes toward me and cocked his head.

"I'd never not respect you, Julie. You're the most respectful girl I know."

Maybe he loves me. I knew I loved him, even if he did make grammatical mistakes. I loved the way he smelled, the way his hands moved over me, and most of all, I loved his kissing. I was positive he kissed better than anybody on earth, even though he was the only boy I'd ever *really* kissed.

"You promise you won't think I'm bad?" I whispered, leaning back into his arms.

"I promise."

He moaned, himself, as we kissed and squirmed on the itchy blanket. Before I realized what was happening, his hand inched up under my skirt, past my knee.

"This is the present I promised you," he whispered. "Happy Birthday, sweet sixteen."

Frances Latimer's words jangled in my head. "Once a boy gets in your pants, you go ahead and go all the way."

CHAPTER 24
THE PANTRY RAID

"He's just a 'good ole boy,' bound by the code of male ethics to try," Frances Latimer said the next day after I told her I'd put on the brakes with Farrel. I hadn't intended to tell her a thing, but she'd picked and weaseled until, finally, she got out of me all the details of my date with Farrel.

"If a girl says no, do you think the boy will ever call back?"

Frances chewed her lower lip. "It depends."

"On what?"

"How long he's willing to keep trying if he never makes it to third base."

My cheeks burned with shame. "I don't know what the bases are."

Frances laughed. "I was afraid of that. Okay, first base is kissing. Shall I go on?"

The long, hot days dragged by, and Farrel didn't call. I looked for him at the Dairyette, but he was never there.

I spent my days in turmoil, afraid if I went out I'd miss Farrel's call, and afraid if I stayed in and answered, it would be my father. Needless worry. It didn't ring. I checked several times to make sure it still had a dial tone.

Mama said, "If you want the phone to ring, sit on the pot or get in the bathtub."

"If I could invent a phone you could carry anywhere you went, I'd make a fortune," I said.

Mama clucked her tongue. "You young'uns and your crazy ideas."

One morning, it finally rang. I started for it, but snatched back my hand. Surely, I could at least let it ring twice.

"Happy Fourth of July!" rang across the wires.

"Oh. Hi, Frances."

"Don't sound so glad to hear from me."

"I'd forgotten today is the fourth."

"It is, and I'm coming by to get you with hot news. Be ready."

"Sooo?" I said as we were heading uptown fifteen minutes later. "What's the hot news?"

"Sooo, Don is having a party at his house tonight. I need you to help me pull it together."

"A party!" *Surely Farrel will be invited.* "Who all's coming?"

"Don told me who to invite. Only a select few. Don't look so worried, silly. You're on the list. Would I have asked you to help me, if you weren't? Lynn's not, though. Neither is Darcy."

"Why?"

"This is confidential, okay? Don can't stand the way Darcy bounces around all over the place and is *always* so happy, and Lynn makes him feel like she's got the goods on him."

"What goods?"

"Oh, like when he was cheating on me with Emma, Lynn gave him dirty looks."

"Is . . . uh . . . anyone else I know coming to the party?"

"Like Farrel?" She wiggled an eyebrow.

I blushed.

"I invited him, but all he said was he'd try."

We rode along in silence. The crepe myrtle trees were blooming, as they always did around the fourth, decorating the streets of our little town like gigantic bouquets the color of watermelon.

Frances swiped her arm across her forehead. "God, it's hot."

The temperature sign on the bank said 104. And it was only ten a.m.

At the next stop light, I kissed off my pride and asked, "What's he been up to, anyway?"

"Who, Farrel? I know he's been working graveyards at the oil refinery. To get money for school."

Of course! That's why he hadn't called. He couldn't go out if he worked graveyards. How must he feel, doing sweat work at the refinery, when fathers of the guys he ran with, like Don, owned the wells that produced the oil?

"I'm surprised you haven't heard from him," she went on. "He told me he had a good time on y'all's date."

"He did? Oh, I'm so glad."

"Even though you wouldn't let him get in your pants," she added with mischievous eyes.

"Oh no! Tell me he didn't say that."

She laughed. "Just testing to see if you did—let him. You're really snowed over him, aren't you? There you go, blushing away. It's okay. I'm snowed over Don, too. So the boys tonight'll be Don, of course, and Farrel, Justin, and Bob, Don's cousin who's visiting from Paragould."

"What girls, besides you and me?"

Her smile lit her face. "Maylene and Laura. You've heard of panty raids, right? Where the college boys go to a girls' dorm and raid it for panties? Well, we're going to have a pan*try* raid, to get the ingredients for homemade ice cream. We'll have a blast. Now, let's see. Maylene puts on that sugary, fake drawl that makes her sound like she doesn't have two brain cells to rub together to get a spark. They must have plenty of sugar."

I screamed with laughter.

"Right on, huh?" she said. "Laura's a cold fish. That's why she never gets asked out twice by the same boy. We'll borrow the ice cream freezer from her."

"Perfect," I said.

"We'll get the cream from your mama, since you're sweeter 'n' cream and pure as driven snow."

"Am I?" I arched one eyebrow.

She looked sly. "You told me yourself, you drew the line with Farrel."

"What'll we get from your house?" I asked.

"Ice cream salt, 'cause I'm a salty kind of gal. And that's the list of girls, unless," she threw me a mischievous look, "you want me to ask Carmen."

"What if Farrel brings her to the party?"

"He won't. I told him I'm inviting the guests." Frances gave me a warning look. "Don't start getting possessive about Farrel. In case you haven't figured it out yet, he's not the type to go steady."

"Maybe that's because he's never been in love before."

She looked surprised. "Before? You've had one date with him and no call since. In my book, that doesn't spell love."

"He kisses me like he loves me."

"Boys kiss the way they kiss. It doesn't matter who the girl is."

"I don't kiss all boys the same way."

"How many boys have you kissed, and I mean *really* kissed?"

I looked away from her. "Just one."

She laughed.

"But still, I can't believe Farrel kisses other girls the way he kisses me."

"That's because you're a girl. To a guy, all cats are gray in the dark."

"Frances! That's horrible."

"Horrible, maybe, but true. Get hip, kid."

Getting dressed that evening, I pulled the elastic neckline of my white peasant blouse down around my shoulders. The thought tripped across my mind that at least, if Farrel and I got together after the party, he wouldn't have to undo any buttons. A tingling warmth set me to giggling. I gave my cheek a gentle slap.

In the backseat of Frances's car, Laura steadied the ice cream freezer, packed to the brim with salt and ice.

"Love your blue birthday skirt," she said.

We picked up Maylene and headed for Don's. On the way, I bit a fingernail to the quick, worrying that Farrel might not be there. It had been eleven whole days since our date. Way too long for a boy to go without calling, if he really liked a girl.

The DeAngelo house was a rambling ranch, set way back off the street at the end of a tree-lined, winding drive. I held my breath as we rounded the final curve. There it sat—the blue Chrysler Imperial.

Farrel stood in a typical "guy huddle" with Justin and Don in the living room. They wore crisp, short-sleeved sport shirts and casual slacks. His face brightened when our eyes met.

"It took y'all long enough to get here."

"We had to bring the ice cream," Frances told him. "Would one of you gents get it out of the car?"

On his way out the door, Farrel gave me what I thought was a special smile, until he gave Laura and Maylene the same one.

A boy introduced as Don's cousin brooded alone in a corner chair. With his ducktail haircut and the cigarette pack rolled up in his T-shirt sleeve, he looked like a James Dean freak.

The house had a kitchen floor of red-and-black checkerboard tiles and modern furniture throughout. Don's mother opened the oven door, and the aroma of brownies drew the crowd to the kitchen. Frances and I dished up the ice cream, and Don served up the cokes.

Ignoring me, Farrel took his dessert outside, where he joined Maylene and Justin on the low brick wall of the terrace. The three of them instantly fell into intense conversation, shutting everyone else out. Without the courage to butt in, I slunk over to the wrought-iron table on the opposite side of the terrace, where I ended up stuck with Laura and Cousin Bob.

In a new yellow sundress that showed more than a little of her cleavage, Frances cracked jokes as she swooped around refilling our drinks.

"I can tell by the way y'all are eating, you don't have lockjaw, but why are you so quiet?"

Cousin Bob talked in a "Brando" mumble that was so soft we had to lean toward him to hear. Once I caught Farrel looking at me, but he quickly went back to his conversation with Justin and Maylene.

After dessert, Mrs. DeAngelo called to us from inside, "Come on, kids. We're gonna have a songfest!"

Frances made the throw up sign. Maylene put on her "please-the-grown-ups" smile. Exchanging looks of dread, the rest of us straggled in and gathered around the piano.

Mrs. DeAngelo belted out an old forty's song, like she was auditioning for the high school musical. We kids made halfhearted efforts to sing along. Don's face flared when Frances moved behind his mother's back and crossed her eyes. Farrel made a few gravelly attempts at finding the notes, then gave up, staring glassy-eyed out the patio doors.

Banging the keys in a grand finale, Mrs. DeAngelo said, "Now, how about some suggestions from you kids?"

"I suggest we go to the country club for the fireworks," Don said.

Farrel jammed his hands in his pockets and looked at the floor.

"You're all my guests," Don said. "How about it, Farrel, my man?"

Farrel pressed his lips tight before giving Don a brief nod.

Justin put an arm around Maylene. Don pulled Frances close. The way Farrel had acted all night made it anyone's good guess whether he wanted to be with Laura or me.

Unable to bear watching Laura pose and twist and bat her eyelashes at him, I stared down at my hands resting on the edge of the piano. When I glanced up, Cousin Bob was headed straight for me. *Please, God, help!* Strong hands gripped my waist.

"Justin and Maylene, y'all want to come with us in my car?" Farrel rested his chin on the top of my head.

Relief and joy surged through me. Cousin Bob executed a sharp pivot and took off toward Laura, whose lower lip began to tremble.

I shoved to the subterranean recesses of my mind the reality that Farrel hadn't called. He'd chosen me. He liked me. I knew he did, whether he called or not. He might even be in love with me. One thing sure: I was in love with him. Tonight we would see skyrockets together under the stars, and maybe even make some of our own.

CHAPTER 25
All Shook Up

July 9, 1956
Dear Elvis,
Can I tell you a secret? I met someone who's got me all shook up. I'm
crazy wild mad about him. The trouble is, I don't know if he feels the
same way about me. Mama doesn't like him, but she never likes anyone,
except Dilberts.

Elvis, your music plays all the time at my house and at the Dairyette.
The young people love it because, like I told you, it's different. Even
preachers are talking about it, but what they say isn't so good. I don't
understand why grown-ups think rock 'n' roll music will cause us to
rebel. But in spite of all that, you'll get to the top, I'm sure. In fact, you're
already there!
Fondly,
Juliet

It didn't take him long to answer.

Dear Juliet,
I was so glad to get your letter, even though you did say you're two-timing
me. Ha! Seriously, though, I'm glad you found yourself a "beau-lover," as
my country friends would say, and that he's got you "all shook up." (Hey,
that'd make a good title for a song!) My advice to you is, play hard to get.
Remember the old saying: "You don't chase the bus you're riding." If he

don't treat you right, let me know, and I'll come down there and give him the old one-two.

I'm enclosing a copy of "Hound Dog," the song I had to sing to a dog, so you'll have it early and be the most "with it" girl in your crowd. On the flip side is "Don't Be Cruel." Let me know how you like them. And you, little Juliet, don't be cruel to me. Write. I love hearing from "real" folks, and you're the most real thing in my life right now.
Elvis

I hid the letter in a place where I was sure Mama would never find it.

Three long weeks went by after the pantry raid party before Farrel called again. On our second official date, we did our usual routine—the drive-in, where we kissed through the entire movie, and then the woods, where we kissed until time for me to go home. I let him unbutton my blouse and play, as he called it, without saying a word, and although I dreaded making him angry if I had to stop him, he didn't once try to go any further.

In the driveway, he turned off the motor and looked at me.

"I'm leaving town tomorrow, and not just for Magnolia."

"Where are you going?"

"Fort Polk, in Louisiana."

"Whatever for?"

"National Guard Camp. For two weeks."

"Two weeks?" I exclaimed, wondering how I could live without him for so long and quite forgetting that it had been over three weeks between the Fourth of July and our second official date.

"Will you write me?" he asked.

"Do Southerners eat cornbread?" *Oops, that was hardly following Elvis's advice.* "I mean, I will, if you write me first."

At the door, he scribbled the address on a gum wrapper and said, "Be good, and don't do anything I wouldn't do."

With a quick kiss, he was gone.

Mama looked up from her book as I plopped down on one of the red couches.

"He's gone for two whole weeks."

When she didn't reply, I went on, "To National Guard Camp. I don't know how I can bear it."

Still, she said not a word, but kept her eyes fixed on me.

"Except he did say he'd write. Oh, Mama, I'm so happy. I think he might love me a little, too."

"I should certainly hope so," Mama said in an icy tone.

From across the room, I couldn't tell whether she was looking at my face or somewhere else. On the way home, I had cleaned up my smeared lipstick, so it couldn't be that. I broke out in a sweat under her unswerving gaze. Abruptly, she slammed her book down on the coffee table and strode out of the den.

When I heard her making noises in the kitchen, I skedaddled to my room and shut the door. The mirror of my dresser told all. Farrel had redone my blouse in the darkness of the woods, and the buttons were catawampus.

There was no getting away from Mama. Seconds later, she flung open the door of my room.

"Julia Lawrence Morgan, you are not to go out with Mr. Budrow ever again. And if you think you might be in any kind of trouble . . ." She broke off, giving me a frightened, apprehensive look.

Her words transformed me into the world's greatest actress— and liar.

"Oh, you mean my blouse? Nothing happened with Farrel, if that's what you're thinking. He's a perfect gentleman. I spilled 7-Up all down my front at the drive-in and had to go to the ladies' room to sponge it out. I just didn't get it buttoned up right, that's all. I wondered why Farrel kept cutting his eyes away the rest of the night. He's such a gentleman. You surely didn't think . . ."

Relief flooded her face. She came to me with outstretched arms.

"I knew you wouldn't let him compromise you," she said, hugging me close. "I'm sorry, darling. I should have trusted you."

"So, I can still go out with him, can't I?"

She hesitated. "I don't think he's good for you, Julie. Elvis is right. You should play a little hard to get."

"Mama, you read my letter!"

"Who, me?" she said with a guilty smile.

I sank down on the bed.

"I thought it was in such a good hiding place. How did you find it?"

"An empty coffee can *was* in a clever hiding place," Mama agreed, "but not in the deep freeze. I'd never put coffee there."

At least she finally thought Elvis was right about something. Maybe the world was on the verge of ending. My own little world was, but I didn't know it yet.

CHAPTER 26
Hound Dog

While Farrel was gone, Carmen called Maylene and asked her to go with her to the Dairyette. That went over like a lead balloon with Maylene, but for me, it further confirmed that Mama was right about Carmen's motive for insisting that we were kin.

On the day Farrel was due back home from National Guard Camp, Eugene Hoffmeyer called. I was babbling a cooked-up excuse not to go out with him, when Mama passed by the phone and handed me a note.

"If you want to keep dating Mr. Budrow, you'd best accept Eugene for tonight."

So I did.

"That's blackmail," I said to her when I hung up.

"I don't want you to get serious over any one boy, especially one who doesn't care enough to write you, after saying he would."

Two seconds later, the mailman came. Lying in the box was a letter from Farrel. I waved it in her face.

"You spoke too soon."

The corners of Mama's mouth turned down. She scowled at me from knitted brows.

"So I did, but you must admit, it's about time."

"You're so critical of him. Sometimes I think it's only because you know how much I like him."

"Maybe it is, partly," she admitted. "I'm only trying to protect you."

"From what?"

She touched my cheek. "How can I say this? Just spit it out, I guess. In my opinion," she took a breath, "he doesn't behave as though he cares as much for you as you do for him."

Deep down, I knew she was right, but I couldn't bear to face it.

"I also think things might improve between you if he didn't get everything he wants, the minute he wants it."

"He doesn't," I said, hoping she couldn't read in my mind the memory of Farrel trying to put his hand up my skirt.

"The minute he says 'frog,' you jump. And I haven't noticed you ever turning him down for a date."

"He hasn't asked often enough!"

"My point exactly. Weeks go by between his calls. That doesn't spell love, my dear."

I resolved to zip my lips with Mama from now on.

"You turn down Eugene without a second thought," she said.

"That's different."

"But look at the results. You've got him dancing on a string."

"I don't want Eugene, especially dancing. He stomps on my toes."

Mama sighed and headed for the kitchen.

It had been a struggle, but I'd held out and not written Farrel first. And now I was holding a letter from him right in my own two hands. I kissed the envelope and tore it open. The letter, written in pencil, made me ecstatic—except for one thing.

Dear Julie,

It feels like I've been gone a year. It's hell doing Guard drills in this Louisiana heat. Right now I'm in the hospital for dehydration. I thought you were going to write me! Being at Guard camp makes a guy crazy to hear from a pretty girl. When I get back, I'll teach you how to play poker.

Well, I hate to cut it so short, but I'm on my back trying to write this, and anyway, that's all that's happened since I seen you last. Write me!
Love,
Farrel

"Love!" I danced around the room. "He signed it 'love'!"

The part that didn't make me ecstatic was "…since I seen you last." If Mama got her hands on this letter, she absolutely would never let me go out with him again. There wasn't a safe place in the house to hide it. I'd have to keep it with me at all times. I tucked it in my purse and thought, if I could somehow trick Eugene into making a grammatical mistake, in writing, I could show it to Mama and be rid of him.

That night he insisted on taking me to the Rialto to see *The Eddy Duchin Story*, a sad movie that made me want to major in music at college. He fumbled for my hand during the show, but I kept it out of his reach. After the movie, I made him take me straight home.

As I was trying to shoo him off at the door, Mama, the eavesdropping witch, materialized and invited him in. I knew that, once he got his rear end plunked down in the living room, he'd be there for hours.

"Julie, sit next to Eugene on the couch," Mama said. "Don't you youngsters know anything about spooning?"

To his credit, even Eugene crossed his eyes.

The windows behind the couch were wide open and the curtains pulled back to let in any hint of a breeze. I was almost lulled to sleep by the whir of the ceiling fan, coupled with Eugene's droning voice, when the heavy grinding of truck gears sounded out front, accompanied by cheering and shouting. Neither Mama nor Eugene paid any attention to the clamor going on outside.

"Stay here and keep Mama company, Eugene," I said, jumping up. "I'll be right back."

I dashed out onto the front porch. A convoy of Army trucks, bringing the cheering National Guard boys home from Fort Polk, was rolling by our house, which sat on the road to South Louisiana. I jumped up and down, waving like total fury. There was no way I could pick out Farrel among the exuberant guys crammed into the trucks, but maybe he would see me.

Mama rushed out with Eugene on her coattail.

"What are you doing?"

"Welcoming home our National Guard boys."

"You're making a spectacle of yourself."

Her face reflected the scornful indignation she nurtured in her debutant soul to use against anyone who made a social faux pas.

I gave Eugene a push toward the door. I didn't want Farrel to see him.

"Go back inside."

Resisting, he threw one arm around me and wagged the other in the air.

"Let's all wave to them."

I tried to squirm away, but he held on fast. It wasn't until Mama ordered us back inside that I escaped his grip. He stayed another whole hour. I survived it by telling myself, "Tomorrow night, I'll be with Farrel."

But Farrel didn't call the next morning.

"He's sleeping late," I told myself.

Noon came and went. No call. When he hadn't called by five p.m., Maylene and I decided the best plan was to go riding around that night and look for him.

The Dairyette parking lot was jammed. The blue Chrysler Imperial was there, but empty. Frances and Don sat as close as two pieces of broken glass glued back together in his father's black Buick. The dented Chevy with peeling mauve paint was also there, parked in front of the concession windows.

"Look, Maylene. Carmen is here, and I see Farrel's car, but where is he?"

"He's right there." Maylene pointed. "See him standing beside Don's car? And look, Justin is waving to us from the backseat. Let's go talk to them."

I got out of the car and gazed across the parking lot at Farrel. He had a remote look on his face as he watched me walking toward him. I had taken only a few steps when he looked over at Carmen, sitting alone in her car, and strode off in her direction.

"This is incredible. He's going over to talk to *her*," I exclaimed.

He leaned into the window on the passenger side, then opened the door and crawled inside the mauve Chevy.

"I cannot believe this!"

"Don't yell," Maylene said, gripping my arm.

"My God, she's starting her car. He's driving away with her." Stunned, I watched the car spin off down the highway. "Maylene," I choked through the swelling in my throat, "he left with her. Farrel *left* with her."

Maylene gave my arm a little shake. "Get a grip. You can't let Frances and them see you like this. Now, we're going right over there and find out what this is all about."

As we walked across the gravel parking lot to Don's car, the jukebox blasted out with "Hound Dog." I could hardly hold up my head. Just this morning, I had told Frances that I thought Farrel must like me a lot to write me from camp. She'd surely told Don, and maybe even Justin. What must they think now, seeing him run off with another girl—especially *that* girl?

My cheeks burned as I leaned against Don's car and listened to the others yak it up about nothing. I knew Maylene was biding her time for just the right moment. During a lull in the chatter, she finally asked, "Why did Farrel leave with that Carmen girl?"

Silence.

At last, Justin spoke up. "Frances bet him five bucks he couldn't go all the way with her."

I came to life. "Frances, you didn't! Why would you do that, when you know . . . he and I . . . ?"

"Two dates don't mean you're going with him. I did it as a joke. Plus, I thought we'd find out what she's like. Don't be ticked at me. Maylene's the one who told me Carmen has hot pants for him."

I turned to Maylene in disbelief. "You told Frances that?"

She flushed.

"I have to go home," I said.

"Don't worry, Julie," Frances said. "Even if he does get her to go all the way, you two look so much alike, he'll probably just pretend it's you. Hang around, and let's find out who wins the bet?"

"You can let us know tomorrow," Maylene said, avoiding my eyes.

Back in her car, she, too, spun out of the Dairyette, while I rode zombie-like, unable to make my brain believe what had happened.

"Peel some rubber, why don'tcha!" yelled some boy from some car somewhere in the parking lot as the last notes of "I Was the One" faded into our background.

"Why did you tell Frances that?" I asked as we sped down the road.

"I never dreamed she'd pull such a stunt. If you're going to be mad, then I really have to question our friendship."

I couldn't lose Maylene.

She looked across the car seat at me. "Before we go home, do you want to turn around and circle the Dairyette again? Maybe they're back, and if they are, then it didn't really mean anything."

We circled the Dairyette at least a dozen more times that night. It was eleven thirty when we at last left the parking lot to go home. Farrel's car was still there, empty, and the mauve Chevy was nowhere to be seen.

The jukebox was playing the flip side of "Hound Dog"—"Don't Be Cruel."

CHAPTER 27
Don't Be Cruel

The next day, Frances told us, "We don't know who won the bet. Farrel and Carmen still weren't back when Don and I left the Dairyette at midnight."

I didn't hear a thing from Farrel that week, and he was never at the Dairyette. I read his letter over and over, trying to figure out what was wrong between us.

Even though school wouldn't start until Tuesday after Labor Day, the band began practice for football season a week earlier. On the top floor of the school building, the band hall simmered at eighty-nine degrees that last week of August.

At the first rehearsal, I was warming up my clarinet when Farrel walked through the door. I kept my face calm, while inside I flipped out. He weaved his way through the chairs and sat next to Don in the trombone section.

Mr. Nesbitt picked up his baton and tapped it on the music stand.

"Boys and girls, we have a visitor this morning—a former band member. Let's welcome Farrel Budrow."

Farrel stood up and did a comedic, showoff bow as we applauded.

At the break, I was standing with our crowd when he came up to us and joined in the small talk. The girls flirted with him like crazy—and he flirted back. He ignored everything I said and wouldn't look at me.

Hating to be a part of the group cackling over him, I had just turned to go back to my seat when Frances asked the big question.

"Did I win the bet about you and Carmen?"

I stopped cold and looked straight at him.

Farrel shot Frances a "shut up" look.

"The bet's no secret," she said.

"You told?" His face took on a greenish cast.

She smirked. "Word has a way of spreading."

He dashed his palm against his forehead.

"So, did you get her to go all the way?" Frances asked.

He gave a feeble laugh. "You know I don't kiss and tell."

"Are you going with that Carmen girl, Farrel?" Maylene asked.

"No!" he said, finally looking straight at me.

After the break, as Mr. Nesbitt tapped his baton on the podium and raised his arms to conduct, something caused me to glance up. Farrel was looking over at me. His gaze was warm. He tilted his head and smiled—his old, familiar smile—and in the midst of the crowded band hall, we were alone together.

Later, at the Dairyette, the soda jerk had just raised the screen to hand me a coke when Farrel came up to me at the concession window.

"I'll take care of this," he said, and putting my money back in my hand, he steered me off to one side. "So, what's the good word?"

I steadied my voice so he couldn't tell I was trembling.

"You must be glad to be home from guard camp."

"You bet. The trouble is, I've had to work graveyards every night and haven't been able go anywhere."

"You were here the first night you were home. You saw me coming over to talk, and you took off with Carmen."

He looked sideways. "Yeah, well, you know what that was about."

His eyes took in the entire parking area as "Don't Be Cruel" rang out around us.

"Are you mad at me about something?" I asked.

His lips tightened. "Why would I be mad at you?"

"I don't know, but like Elvis's new song says, 'Don't Be Cruel.'"

"You think too much about Elvis," he said. "You think too much, period. And I'm not being cruel."

"How can a person think too much?" My voice broke. "And why would you go out with another girl your first night home, after you wrote to me?"

"There's one thing you need to learn," he said. "I'm gonna do what I want to when I want to! And I didn't go out with Carmen, we went to the woods."

I stood there, feeling like he'd slapped my face, and watched him walk away.

"Farrel," I called.

He threw an annoyed look at me over his shoulder. "What?"

I wanted to beg him to tell me why he was so mad, but the only words I could get past my lips were, "Thanks for the coke."

"De nada," he replied.

The only other person I knew who said "de nada" was Carmen.

CHAPTER 28
Love Me Tender

The next day, I asked Frances to help me plan a poker party for Labor Day Weekend.

"Don'll love that. He and Farrel are always playing poker."

"I want Farrel to come, but I think he's mad at me."

"What about?" she asked.

"I don't know. He might not come if I invite him."

"He'll be devastated if you have a party and don't invite him."

"I know," I said. "Could you get Don to ask him?"

"Done."

The afternoon of the party, she and I were about to stir up Mama's recipe for pimento cheese when Don arrived for the party—three hours early—with Farrel in tow.

"We came to help out," Farrel said.

Instant delirium! But I played it cool.

"You'll need to wear these," I said, giving them each an apron.

When I looked back at Farrel, he had his tied around his head, which set us howling. I helped him get it on right, handed him the grater and the cheese, and gave Don a fork to mash the pimentos.

"Do you care if some of my fingertips get grated into this cheese?" Farrel asked, laughing.

I was adding mayonnaise when Don said, "The Razorback football game in Fayetteville this afternoon is on TV."

Ever the eavesdropper, Mama called from the den, "I've got it on already."

Don and Frances hunkered down with her to watch the game. Farrel sat with me at the breakfast room table to help spread sandwiches.

"Heard from your boyfriend lately?" he asked.

"Who do you mean?"

"Got so many you can't keep 'em straight?" A flicker of anger crossed his face, which he immediately replaced with a smile. "I mean Elvis the Pelvis. Is he still beating down your door?"

I reached across him to get more bread. Our arms touched. He looked at me with the same expression of hunger he wore with me at the drive-in.

"Elvis is out in Hollywood, shooting a movie—*Love Me Tender.*"

"Whoa! He *is* climbing up in the world. Do I put mayonnaise on both sides of the bread?"

"Just one. He sends me records all the time, but we've never been more than friends."

"Go, Hogs, go!" Frances yelled.

"Y'all are missing a great game," Don called to us.

"What about your other boyfriend?" he asked, his mouth taut.

"You can't mean Eugene Hoffmeyer."

He looked quizzical.

"The nerd I went to the Valentine Dance with—after you didn't call?"

"All right, touché. But I mean the guy on the porch with you the night I came home from guard camp. I couldn't believe you were out there waving at us . . . me . . . with his arm around you."

I dropped my voice low. "Mama blackmailed me. She said I couldn't go out with you anymore if I didn't go with him that night."

He stopped slathering pimento cheese on a slice of bread and looked at me with sudden comprehension.

"Ahhh. So that was it."

Going against Mama's catechism of never talking about anything important, I said, "Why did you go off with Carmen that next night, Farrel?"

"Just figure that's what happens when you don't answer a person's letter."

"Farrel, I didn't get your letter until the day you got home."

"Tell that to the judge."

I looked straight into his eyes. "No, really. I swear."

"That's odd, since I wrote it the first week I was there."

"Don't you know I would have written you back if there had been time?" I didn't like the pleading note in my voice, but I wanted him to believe me. "Maybe mail is slow in and out of an Army place like that."

He furrowed his brow. "No sweat. Maybe I mailed it later than I thought."

"Is that why you didn't call?"

"I was beat after two weeks of playing war. I figured it was too late to call, anyway, by the time I woke up that afternoon. Since then, I've been up to my ears."

"With what? Trying to get Carmen to go all the way so you can win the bet?"

"You bet." He laughed.

I didn't find it funny. I focused hard on the sandwich I was making and said nothing.

He put a cheese-smeared hand over mine.

"I couldn't afford to pay Frances five dollars if I lost the bet," he said, "so I tried, but Carmen told me, 'Tough titties.' We didn't do a thing but sit out there in the woods talking until nearly one o'clock in the morning. I'm trying to convince Frances that I won so I won't have to pay up, so don't tell her, okay? Let's you and me forget it. Be with me at the party tonight, and tomorrow night we'll go to the movies."

I wanted to shout and dance and fly in the wind, and I wanted him to take me where everyone could see us together.

"Can we go to the Rialto to see *The King and I*?"

He squeezed my hand. "We're going to the drive-in. I'd tell you it's not just because I want to feel you up, but it is."

"Shush," I hissed. "Mama'll hear you."

"Wooo pig sooie!" whooped Mama, Frances, and Don.

"Call those Hogs!" Farrel sang out, and with a quick glance into the den to make sure they were paying no attention to us, he leaned close and planted on me what I had come to call his kiss of love.

The whole crowd and their dates came to the party. Mama brought out her poker chips but would only let us play for match sticks.

Farrel kept me beside him all night. At the poker table, he showed me his hands, sometimes letting me choose which cards to keep and which to discard.

It was about eight thirty, during a tense moment of the game, when I heard a knock at the front door.

"Who could that be?" Maylene asked. "Isn't everyone here that you invited?"

"Keep on playing," I said, slipping out of my chair. "I'll answer it."

The front door was open, but Mama had hooked the screen before going to her room to leave the rest of the house to us kids. Bugs bobbed and flitted in a frenzied dance around the white porch light. I peered through the slack screen. My father stood on the porch, swatting at gnats and candle flies.

CHAPTER 29
My Baby Left Me

My heart pounded against my ribs at the sight of him. Fragmented memories of the iron pipe and broken glass swept through my mind.

"The bugs are driving me nuts. Why in the name of Pete don't you have a yellow bug light up here?"

I could only shake my head.

"Get it," he said. "I'll put it up."

I glanced toward Mama's closed bedroom door, praying she was asleep.

"No, thanks. I don't need any help."

He gave me a cynical smile. "I thought you were going to call."

"I haven't had time."

"You never came to visit me. Never called. Nothing. Come with me to the Coffee Cup for a piece of pie."

"Now?" I sputtered.

"Yes, now."

"I can't."

"Why not?"

"The house is full of people."

As if on cue, laughter and happy talk reverberated from the breakfast room.

"Is Elizabeth having a party?"

"No, I am."

He gave a half laugh. "I keep forgetting you're practically a grown young lady."

I didn't know what to say, so I studied his face, which I had not seen closely for months. Gray muted his sideburns and brows, and lines had crept around his eyes. His faded, brown jacket was threadbare at the elbows. But I smelled no alcohol, and his speech was not thick tongued.

"I didn't mean to bust in. I had to see you, even if it was just for a minute." His face brightened. "Come by the house tomorrow afternoon. Your grandmother baked all day today. It's pumpkin pie weather. We'll sit at the table in the kitchen and have a piece. Better yet, come right after church. You can have Sunday dinner with us. Mom promised Pop chicken and dumplings. They want to see you so bad."

Maybe I should go for a visit tomorrow. Maybe I could talk to him about Farrel, like Maylene talks to her dad about guys.

He searched my face, like a cat stalking a fly.

"Please come, honey."

The remembrance of Mama's warning that men folks in my father's family were spawned from violence jarred me back to reality. I must be insane to think of doing such a thing. Mama would have a fit. On the other hand, I knew from the few visits I'd had with him, my grandmother's pies were fantastic.

I curled my cold fingertips inside my palms and swallowed.

"I don't know. I'll have to see."

He glanced down and mumbled, "I know your mother's at the bottom of this. She's poisoned you against me."

My heart missed a beat.

"What? I can hardly hear you."

He spoke up. "Tell Elizabeth to expect a court summons. I'll sue her so fast it'll make her head spin. I'll win, too, according to His Honor, the judge, because she's defied my court-ordered visitation rights."

"It's not her fault."

"Then whose fault is it?"

"Mine."

"If that's so, I expect you to be there tomorrow."

"I need to get back to my party," I said, checking again that the hook on the screen door was fastened.

"Sure," he said, "but remember this. It's your choice—a visit or a court summons."

I watched him strut down the walkway and disappear into the night. That seemed to be our history—me watching him disappear into the night. Something about it made me hurt in the deepest part of my being. I couldn't imagine why.

I didn't go to visit him the next day, and I didn't tell Mama about his threat. I'd deal with that when and if the court summons came. Instead, I tried to focus on doing my nails and looking my best for my date with Farrel, but I couldn't help glancing at the door every few minutes, in case my crazy father showed up on the doorstep again.

That night at the drive-in, Farrel pulled me close and said, "I have to go back to school pretty soon. As a sophomore, I'll have to study more and won't get to come home so often. I want to make tonight special— the last one of the summer—one we'll always remember."

I looked deep into his eyes. "Being together makes it special already. I love you, Farrel."

I thought he'd say he loved me, too, but he only squeezed me tight and whispered in my ear, "Let's skip the Dairyette tonight and go straight to the plum tree."

The tiniest nip of autumn was in the air, but there was no leisurely moment to enjoy it. Once at the plum tree, Farrel was stricken with an acute case of wandering hands. I let him undo my blouse, but when he reached up my skirt, I shoved against his hand.

"Don't, Farrel."

"Julie, you're so beautiful."

I warmed to his words, but the second I relaxed my hold on his hand, it rushed up under my skirt again, this time past my knees.

"Don't," I whispered.

"Your pal Elvis ought to sing a song called 'Don't.' We could listen to it and you wouldn't have to keep saying it over and over."

He moved his hand upwards again.

"Stop, please, stop," I said, this time using all my strength to push his hand away."

"Don't you want to?"

I held his face in my hands and looked into his eyes.

"It doesn't matter what I want, we can't."

We kissed for a while, then he tried again, and again I pushed him away, until a silent battle ensued between his hand moving up and mine pushing it away.

"I thought you loved me," he murmured in my ear.

"I do."

His hand shot up all the way.

With all my strength, I shoved it down.

"Stop it right now, or take me home."

Without missing a beat, he sat up and started the car.

My voice broke as he gunned it and peeled off the gravel road onto the highway.

"It's too big a risk, Farrel."

"Yup."

"Don't be mad. I don't think either one of us is ready to get married yet."

"Yet?" He gave a short laugh and flicked a slow-eyed glance toward me. "Julie, learn one thing: Hell'll freeze over before I get married."

The shock of his words flushed through me, but I managed to keep my voice light.

"My point exactly."

We didn't say another word all the way to the house. He walked me to the door and wheeled around to leave.

"Wait, Farrel."

He turned, a quizzical look on his face.

"What I said is true. I do love you."

His eyes opened slightly from their half-mast position, and he looked at me for a long moment.

"Know what my motto is? Don't tell me, show me."

Farrel went back to school without even calling to say goodbye.

At the first football game of the season, our Wildcats played the Camden Panthers. Driving to the game, I flipped the radio on, and Elvis's rich voice singing "My Baby Left Me" filled the car. Somehow, he and I were connected in this universe. Each time he gave the world a new song, it related exactly to the path my life was taking.

During the game, Maylene and I looked out from between the purple and white streamers decorating the bandstand and spotted Farrel sitting in the bleachers.

"He came home for the game," I said. "Is he alone?"

She squinted. "Looks like."

After the band's halftime show, I weaved my way through the crowds of people, milling around in the concession area with their hotdogs and cold drinks. When I spotted him, he was only three or four feet away. He took a step toward me.

"I didn't know you were coming home this weekend."

"I wasn't sure I was," he said.

"Are you going . . . ?" I hesitated.

"Going where?" he asked.

"To the dance after the game."

He gazed off into the crowd, and a frown grew between his brows. In the distance, I heard the band starting the number to launch the second half. I was late but completely incapable of leaving before we had a chance to talk.

"Shouldn't you be getting back?" His face was concerned. His voice, kind.

"In a minute." I tried to smile, as if our conversation was totally normal. "So do you want to go—to the dance?"

"If the Wildcats don't win, there's no reason to celebrate. With the score twenty-one to nothing now, it doesn't look promising."

"The dance'll be fun, whether we win or not," I said, hating the pleading note in my voice.

He looked off into the distance, like he was trying to decide. Finally, he said, "I usually drop by. If I do, save me a dance, will you?" And he was gone.

I broke and ran all the way back to the bandstand.

Seizing my clarinet, I yanked the pieces apart and slammed them into the indentations inside the case.

"I've got to get out of here," I told Maylene.

She gripped my arm. "You can't. Now sit down, and don't make a scene."

The stadium lights, the hubbub, the dissonant squawking of band instruments—everything seemed unreal.

"Farrel is here, and he won't take me to the dance. I'm leaving."

She put out a restraining hand, like Mama did when I was little and standing up next to her in the car and she had to stop suddenly.

"You can't leave for two reasons. Number one, you can't let him know it means that much to you."

"But—"

"And number two, you'll get an F in band. Then you'll have to go back to taking P.E. and wearing those horrible uniforms that are ten times worse than these."

The thought of P.E. uniforms made me laugh through the tears leaking from my eyes.

"What am I going to do? I think I've lost him."

Her reply came stunningly fast. "Get a boy, any boy, to take you to the dance."

I glanced along the rows of band kids. The only possibility was Eugene Hoffmeyer, whose grinning face looked like a sunflower in the curvature of his sousaphone.

Maylene saw the direction I was looking.

"He's a warm male body. He'll do."

"I cannot go on another miserable date with him. Besides, Farrel knows we're just friends. It wouldn't stir a twinge of jealousy in him."

"Don't do it for Farrel. Do it for yourself."

My mind fractured. I should do something for myself, yes, but what? Visit my father? Go home, wake up Mama, and tell her about his threats? Stay here? Go to the dance by myself? Endure Eugene one more time? Dump Farrel? Give him another chance? What?

"I can't," I said, sagging under the weight of Maylene's disapproving gaze.

She slung her red ponytail.

"Not even to keep running with the in-crowd?"

The next morning, early, I called her.

"Oh, hi, Julie." Her downward tone said she was anything but pleased to hear my voice on the other end. "I've only got a couple of minutes. Mother and I are going to Woolworths."

I glimpsed my anxious face in the mirror on Mama's dresser.

"Farrel came to the dance," she said, "if that's what you're calling about. Alone. You should have done what I told you and gone with old Eugene. Then you could have kept tabs on him yourself."

"You sound so impatient, Maylene."

"I don't have a lot of time to waste talking about Farrel Budrow. I'd blow him off, if I were you, and move on."

"Did he ask where I was?"

"He didn't ask me."

I had no need to look in the mirror. I could feel the shame staining my face. I knew she was right. I should move on, but I couldn't.

I heard her call out through a muffled mouthpiece, "Just a sec, Mother."

I wondered if she was really talking to her mother or just faking it to get off the phone with me.

"I've got to go, Julie," she said, "but I want to tell you one thing. That girl, Carmen, showed up and actually had the audacity to plunk herself down at our table several times last night."

"Oh no."

"Oh, yes. I think she's gotten the idea she can horn in because of her relationship with you."

"I don't have a relationship with her, and you know it."

"Don't get hot with me, Julie. I'm willing to help you as much as I can with Farrel, which isn't much, in my opinion, but Farrel aside, you've got to let that girl know, once and for all, that whatever is between you two, she has got to get rid of the idea she can run with us, because she can't."

I was shaking when I hung up the phone.

CHAPTER 30
Robbing the Cradle

Even without a date, I was the star of the party on Sunday night when the crowd and their boyfriends came over to watch Elvis on *The Ed Sullivan Show*.

"Show them the letter," Frances said when we were all sitting on the floor in the den in front of the television after the show. "Wait'll you get a load of this, gang."

I handed the letter to Maylene, who gave it a fleeting look and passed it on to Justin. The other kids crowded around, hanging over his shoulder and peeking beneath his elbow to read it.

"Whoa!" Justin said. "That dude is going to get fifty thousand dollars for just singing a few songs on TV."

Frances goosed him in the ribs. "It's *The Ed Sullivan Show*, nut wagon."

Justin gave me a broad smile. "Good thing old Farrel isn't here. He'd be big-time jealous over you getting letters like this, signed 'I'll remember you—always, Elvis.'"

"Yeah," Darcy said, lounging against Lynn and looking at me with awe in her eyes. "You're a star, too, Julie. Just by being Elvis's friend, stray sprinkles of his stardust have filtered all over you."

"Oh, puleeze," Maylene said. "Where is 'old' Farrel, anyway?"

I shrugged. I'd been listening for his knock all night and watching the front door, but all I'd seen was bugs bobbing around the porch light. It was so late now, my hope was lost.

"I told him about the party," Don said, glancing at me, then cutting his eyes away. "Maybe he had to study tonight."

"May-bees don't fly in September," Maylene said. "Look, y'all, the news is on. Be quiet. Did you hear what the announcer said? Historic event. Tonight, September ninth, 1956, over sixty million people watched *The Ed Sullivan Show*. And to think, we saw Elvis at the stadium just a year ago and thought he was rinky-dink."

"Here's your letter back," Justin said, handing it to me. "Put it in the safe-deposit box. It'll be worth millions in a few weeks."

My stardom by association had twinkled out by the next morning. I was starting my junior year with no boyfriend and on the slippery edge of acceptance by the in-crowd.

The whole month of October, I heard nothing from Farrel. According to Maylene's unspoken rules, the girls in the group were supposed to have at least one date every weekend. Darcy, Laura, and Lynn always did. Frances and Don went out Friday, Saturday, and Sunday. Maylene had a date with Justin every Saturday night, while I had a date with *The Jackie Gleason Show*.

One November afternoon, as the carpool group piled into Maylene's old crate, the Gray Goose, so called because it was ancient, Frances asked, "Can we stop at Escoubas Cleaners on our way? I need to pick up my dress for the party."

Maylene shot her a look from behind the wheel.

"Uh oh." Frances clapped a hand over her mouth.

No one said a word for what seemed like forever. The one side of Maylene's face I could see turned bright red. Darcy began to hum the school fight song, and Lynn patted my hand resting between us on the backseat.

"Have I missed a chapter somehow?" I finally managed to ask.

"I don't know what you mean," Maylene said, and without pausing for my answer, she burst out with, "Did you all hear the latest? Eugene

Hoffmeyer gave Rhonda a silver heart on a chain and asked her to go steady."

"No!" shrieked Darcy.

I nearly choked. "You are kidding."

"I'm surprised you all didn't know," Maylene said. "She's been sticking it in everybody's face all day."

Frances whipped around to look at me from the front seat.

"That must be music to your ears, huh, Julie?"

"They belong together," Lynn said.

I didn't care—not an iota. But somehow, I felt hollow inside.

The girls babbled without ceasing while Frances ran in at the cleaners. Then, big event—instead of our usual stop at the Dairyette, Maylene headed straight for my house. On the way, it started to drizzle.

I waved backward over my shoulder to keep them from seeing my face as I darted through the now pounding rain to the porch. Inside, doubled over and heaving sobs, I made my way to my room and threw myself on the bed, where I spilled grief so deep my guts ached. Farrel was slipping away, and the girls were obviously hiding something from me. And though I struggled to keep it repressed at the back of my mind, the terror of knowing that any day the court summons from my father might come surpassed everything. The only time I ever had relief from that was on Sundays, when there was no mail.

At last I eased up and gazed out the window. As I watched the rain beating dead leaves into mud, an indisputable fact wormed its way into my brain. Farrel wasn't going to call.

As soon as I thought there had been enough time for her to get home, I telephoned Frances.

"What's up, kiddo?"

"Where's the party?"

"Uh oh. I really let the cat out of the bag, didn't I?"

"Tell me."

"Maylene is having a hump day party."

"When?"

"Tonight, of course. It's Wednesday."

I couldn't speak over the swelling in my throat. I felt numb with shock.

"Promise me you'll blow it off," she said.

"You know I never can. Are you all throwing me out of the carpool, too?"

"Of course not. This party is Maylene's bright idea. None of the rest of us had anything to do with it."

"But why?" My voice caught. "Why would she leave me out? We're best friends."

"There's no one to pair you off with, Julie. Especially now that good old Eugene has been snapped up."

"It's because I haven't heard from Farrel, isn't it?"

She said nothing.

"Frances, have you heard anything . . . I mean . . . from Don, or anybody . . . about Farrel . . . and me?"

I heard her sigh. "Actually, I have."

"What? Tell me."

"You have to promise you won't let on that I told you."

"I promise."

"Don asked Farrel if he wanted to ask you to double with us and go to Little Rock to see the Razorbacks play."

My heart jumped. "And?"

"He said he didn't think so."

"But why?"

"He said . . ." She paused. "Are you sure you want me to tell you this?"

"Yes! I have to know what's going on."

"He said he really likes you, but going with you makes him feel like he's robbing the cradle."

"Robbing the cradle?"

"His words, not mine," she said.

"What did he mean by that?"

"Beats me. Did you have a fight?"

"No. On our last date, everything was fine. I mean, pretty fine . . . until . . ."

Her voice dropped a note. "Until what?"

"Until I wouldn't . . . you know . . ." I broke off.

"Julie, Julie, when are you going to learn how to handle boys?"

The gloom from outside stepped into the room.

"Never, I guess."

"If you want a steady boyfriend, you have to give him what he wants."

"You mean . . . ?"

Silence.

"Frances, are you serious?"

"I'm going to tell you something, Julie, because I like you, and I can't stand to see you hurt like this, but you better not tell a soul. Do you promise?"

"I promise."

"All right, here goes." She took another deep breath. "How do you think I got Don back from our illustrious homecoming queen, Emma Jarvis?"

"I don't know. I guess he—" I cut myself off. "Frances, you don't mean you let him . . . I mean, are you and Don . . . ?"

She was silent again.

"But you could get—"

"I won't," she whispered into the phone. "We use the rhythm method."

"The what?"

"It's a Catholic thing. You just have to count days. It's simple."

"But Frances, you're a Baptist."

"I know. I try not to think about that."

I took a shaky breath. "So, you think Farrel would go with me if I—?"

"Made in the shade. Listen, I gotta get ready for the party. Don't let this eat you up, okay? I'll put my mind to finding another guy for you. That's all you need to stay in the crowd. The truth is, Maylene likes you. She just has an image in her mind of how things ought to be, and the rest of us have to live up to it."

I hung up the phone and stared out the window again. I had to do something, and quick.

CHAPTER 31
SHOW ME

Now was as good a time as any to do it. Mama wasn't home from work yet. I'd have some privacy. Information gave me the number, and with shaky fingers, I dialed Arkansas College. A switchboard operator with a heavy nasal twang answered and transferred me to his dorm. The phone rang twenty-seven times. My stomach churned. Finally, someone picked up the extension.

"Second floor, Hayes."

"Is . . . I mean . . . May I speak with Farrel Budrow?"

"Hold on. Farrel! Phone!" He shouted so loud I had to hold the receiver away from my ear.

I could hear guys yelling and footsteps going past. Endless minutes dragged by. Finally, Farrel's voice said, "Yep?"

"Hi, Farrel."

"Julie! Well, well, this is a first. To what do I owe the honor of a call from you?"

I restrained myself from saying I missed him so much I was nearly crazy.

"Oh, I just wanted to say hi."

"That was nice of you. How's the gang?"

"Fine. Everyone's fine." I glanced at the clock. Five fifteen. Mama would be barreling in any minute.

"How are the fighting Wildcats?" he asked.

"They've won their last few games. Listen, Farrel, I've been doing a lot of thinking lately."

"Hmmm, thinking can become a bad habit. What can I do to keep you from doing that?"

I wanted to say, "You can come home and take me out, kiss me all night, give me your class ring, and tell me you love me—any or all of those." What I did say was, "I'm ready."

"You're ready?"

His voice painted a picture of his puzzled face.

"Yes. I'm ready."

"Ready . . . for what?"

From the window, I saw Mama's car turning into the driveway.

"You said, 'Don't tell me, show me.' I'm ready to show you."

Another silence fell. Mama slammed the car door. I pounded on my thigh, silently screaming for him to hurry up and say something.

"Are you sure?" he finally asked.

"Un-huh, but I can't talk now. Mama's coming in the door. I gotta go."

"Wait! How 'bout we go out this Friday night?"

"Okay," I said.

"Pick you up at seven."

I slammed the phone down just as Mama came inside.

On Friday night, for the first time ever, Farrel took me downtown to the Rialto. I was about to decide that maybe he didn't care anymore if people thought we were going together, when my sensible voice reminded me that the drive-in was closed for the winter.

Elvis's first movie, *Love Me Tender*, was playing.

"You know, this is a real sacrifice for me to sit through your other boyfriend's movie, don't you?" he said with a grin as he gave the cashier a dollar for our two tickets.

My *other* boyfriend. My heart swelled.

"Now that he's a movie star, I think I *will* claim him as a boyfriend."

While we waited for the show to start, I gazed up at the crystal chandelier, my mind in turmoil. Maybe my *saying* I was ready to "show" him would be enough, and he wouldn't make me actually go through with it. Maybe it was just an ego thing with him, especially if he knew Don and Frances were doing it.

He reached over and took my hand. His smile dissolved my fears, until a moment later when he looked past me toward the aisle.

"Maylene and Justin are here," he said.

"Julie!" Maylene called over the heads of people seated between us.

I looked toward her hearty wave and managed a half-smile, hoping they wouldn't come over and sit with us. Justin, balancing popcorn and cokes, managed to navigate them into seats nowhere near us just as the lights dimmed.

"Catch you later," she trilled across the audience as the red velvet curtains hanging over the screen slid apart, their heavy folds barely rippling.

I could hardly believe that the giant figure on the big screen was the same Elvis who, just a year and a month ago, had driven me home. There wouldn't be any more rides in the pink Cadillac. He was a movie star now.

Maylene and Justin pressed through the crowd and caught up with us as the theatre emptied at the end of the show.

"I didn't know y'all had a date tonight," she said in her exaggerated drawl. "You never tell me anything anymore, Julie. Shame on you."

"How ya doin', Justin?" Farrel said, holding out his hand.

Justin shook with him. "Missed you on the golf course this afternoon."

"Couldn't make it home in time," Farrel said, steering me out the lobby doors.

"Y'all come on over and sit in our car at the Dairyette," Maylene said, and without waiting for a response, she tugged on Justin's hand and did a little dance step as they headed toward his father's black Buick.

We skipped the Dairyette. The moon was out in full glory that night. My heart was beating so hard I was sure Farrel could hear it when he stopped the car by the old plum tree and doused the lights.

He immediately got out, went to the trunk, and brought a small cooler back with him.

"I'm having a beer. I brought a coke for you."

"What if I want a beer, too?"

"Do you drink beer?"

"I've never even tasted it, but I'd like to."

"I'll give you a sip, but that's all. You're too young. I have to look out for my girl."

His words warmed me, but the cold beer tasted awful.

"How can you stand that stuff?"

He smiled at me in the moonlit car.

"Still in the same frame of mind about this?"

I couldn't believe I was nodding "yes."

"Not scared?"

"A little. What if . . . ?" My voice was pitched way too high.

He took my hand and kissed my fingers, one at a time.

"You won't get in trouble. I'll use one hundred percent safe protection. Trust me."

He opened the car door and held out his hand to me.

"Let's get in the back seat so the steering wheel won't be in the way."

My sensible voice said, "You need to call this off."

"If you do, you'll lose him for good," my romantic voice argued.

Outside the car, Farrel looked up at the moon, floating high above the plum tree.

"Let's wish on a star."

"The moon is so bright, it's drowning most of them out," I said.

He pointed to a dim star, low on the horizon. "There's one. It must be Venus, Goddess of Love."

"Venus is a planet," I said, feeling like my throat was closing.

He gave me a sad smile. "You know, I'd take you to a nice place, and we'd have champagne and all the trimmings, if I could, don't you?"

I nodded and swallowed hard.

Once we were in back, he cut short our usual kissing, and before I knew it, he had me lying on the seat with my skirt and petticoat pushed up.

Oh God, this is really going to happen.

"Do not go through with this!" sensible ordered.

"Do you want him to think he's 'robbin' the cradle'?" romantic voice hammered in my head.

"Farrel, wait," I whispered. "Someone might drive up and catch us."

"They won't," he said and went straight to the main attraction.

The rest was a painful blur, except for certain moments that would remain with me forever in blazing Technicolor. His frequent glances out the rear window to make sure no one was driving up. The sight of the moon as I looked at it upside down from the window above my head. And the total absence of any words spoken, tender or otherwise.

The whole time it was happening, I could hear Elvis singing low on the radio, "I Want You, I Need You, I Love You." Over and over, I repeated silently to myself, *Now Farrel'll be in love with me.* Elvis's "Heartbreak Hotel" came on at the big moment.

Then it was over. I sat up and looked out the window. The plum tree was still there. The moon, now upright, still sailed through the night clouds. The girl I had been was gone forever.

"It won't hurt the next time," he said.

The next time? It hadn't occurred to me I'd have to do it more than once. I waited for him to say he loved me, or anything that showed he understood how I must be feeling after my first time, but he only lit up a cigarette.

"I'll let you have one drag, if you want it," he said, holding it out to me.

I shook my head. "I didn't know you smoked."

"I usually don't, but you know what they say."

"No, I don't know what they say."

"'A cocktail before and a cigarette after.'"

He leaned back and smoked.

Trembling, I struggled to put myself back together in the dark. Outside, the crickets chirped, and a cloud drifted over the moon.

"I think it's supposed to rain tomorrow," he said, tossing the butt of his cigarette out the window. "Let's go see who's still at the Dairyette."

My heart gave a dull thud. He wasn't going to hold me close. He wasn't going to ask me to go steady. He wasn't going to tell me he loved me. He didn't even look at me like he loved me.

I blinked hard as we got back in the front seat and drove away. I wanted to bawl my eyes out.

On the way to the Dairyette, we passed Justin's house. I knew he and Maylene hadn't done it. That girl had made it perfectly clear she would never do IT before marriage. Stupid me had given away my innocence—not just to win Farrel's love, but to insure my acceptance in *her* crowd.

If only I could turn back time and be again the girl I was before I decided to "show" him.

There he sat, driving along as though nothing out of the ordinary had happened. Just as I was about to conclude that he had only used me, he pulled me over next to him in the car and kissed my fingers.

At the Dairyette, Maylene was out of Justin's car and headed toward us before Farrel even turned off the headlights.

"Where have you all been?" she demanded, narrowing her eyes at me.

Oh God, she'll be able to tell by the look on my face, I thought, trying to appear calm. Everybody's going to know the minute they see me. I remembered what Della, Rhonda, and Faye had said when they tracked down the girl Elvis bought the car for—that a girl who's done IT looks different. When I got out of the car, I stood straight and tall. Slouching was a sure sign.

Farrel got cokes for us, and we sat for a while in Justin's car, listening to the jukebox blaring from the Dairyette. When we got out to return to Farrel's car, Maylene called me back to the passenger window and whispered in my ear.

"There's a small blood stain on the back of your skirt."

I went numb. Shame stained my face.

She stared intently at me. I made myself shrug.

"It's just my 'friend,'" I said and rushed to get in the car.

At my front door, Farrel tucked back a curl of hair that had slipped down on my forehead.

"I'll give you a call. Gotta run, now, honey. Okay?"

I shivered. "But Farrel . . ."

He looked sideways. "Your Mama's probably spying on us. I'll catch up with you later."

I looked at him in disbelief. "Farrel."
"What?" he said in a cross tone.
Wasn't he even going to set another date?
"Is that all you have to say to me after . . . after?"
He looked uncomfortable. "What do you want me to say?"
"That you love me, too."
"Didn't I just show you in the backseat of the car?"

CHAPTER 32
That's When Your Heartaches Begin

Farrel didn't call the next day. Or the next. Or the next. The big Christmas dance was coming up on Saturday night. No one had asked me, of course, but on the Friday before the dance, Maylene still didn't have a date, either.

"Let's go to the Dairyette tonight and see what we can scare up," she suggested that afternoon after school. "I'll pick you up."

Since I'd had another date with Farrel, she was acting like my best friend again. As we headed back to the car with our cokes, she said, "Surely Farrel plans to take you to the dance. Haven't you heard from him?"

"Not a word since . . ." Shock flushed through me.

"Since what?" she demanded, peering hard into my face.

"Last weekend," I said, glossing over my almost slip. Maylene must never find out that I had gone all the way with Farrel. "Where is Justin?" I rushed on. "And why aren't you going with him?"

"His folks have taken him to Princeton to interview for school next year. I have to find another date."

"You would actually go with someone else?"

She flipped her ponytail. "We're not going steady. I can go with someone else if I want to."

"Won't he be upset?"

"So what if he is? Get your priorities straight, Julie. We're young. We should be dating lots of fellows. How else are we going to find the right one?"

Would Farrel be upset if I went to the dance with someone else?

"Too bad about good ole Eugene giving Rhonda his ring," she said. "I expect you might've been willing to put up with him for one night to go to something as important as the Christmas dance. I've never in my whole life not had a date to a dance. What will people think?" She surveyed the parking lot. "I don't see a single soul to flirt with. I'd even go with Steve, if he asked me." She grabbed my arm. "Look. Isn't that Farrel's car pulling in?"

"It is. Oh my God." My heart flopped.

"I don't think he sees us," Maylene said. "Roll down your window."

"Farrel!" I called. He veered toward us, hopped out, and bent to peer in the window on the passenger side.

"Well, look who's here," Maylene said. "The ghost of Christmas past."

"I feel like a ghost. Been studying hard all week." His smile only for me eased my jitters. "What are y'all up to?"

"We're out here hoping to rustle up—"

"Just hanging around," I broke in, giving her a look. "I didn't know if you were coming home."

His eyes flickered guilt. "By the time I got here, I figured it was too late to call. Slide over."

He got in the car and put his arm around me.

"I hear old Justin's gone up to Princeton this weekend," he said.

Maylene clucked her tongue. "He would pick the weekend of the Christmas dance."

"That's tomorrow, isn't it?" Farrel asked.

She flashed him a smile. "Tomorrow's the big night."

For a long time, nobody said a word. Just when I thought I might go totally insane and madly pull my hair out one strand at a time, he mumbled, "I have to go back to Magnolia tomorrow. I left a book in my room I need over the weekend, and my old man has to have the car all day. I'm really up salt creek without a paddle."

I bounced up straight and looked at him.

"You can ride with me. Mama ordered me a Christmas dress from that fancy shop over there, and I have to go get it."

"It's a date," he said with a big smile. "What time will you pick me up?"

I nearly exploded with joy. I'd get to be with him all day, and maybe he'd ask me for a date to the dance.

"How about nine thirty? This is great. I was hoping someone would go with me."

"You didn't ask me," Maylene said. "I'd have gone with you. I want to get some new records, and Magnolia's music store has an ad in the paper for a big sale."

I wanted to scream at her. *Can't you see? This is my chance to be alone with Farrel in the daytime, doing regular things, like people going together do.*

When neither Farrel nor I said anything, she turned doe eyes on us.

"Would you all mind terribly if I tagged along?"

"Uh . . . well, I don't know," I said at the exact same moment Farrel said, "The more, the merrier. I'll treat you girls to a tour of my dorm room."

When I drove up at Farrel's home the next morning, I saw right away that Mama was right. He did live on the wrong side of the tracks—and so close to them that trains must wake the family off and on all night.

The house was shot-gun style, and last summer's flowerpots and rusty gardening tools junked up the yard. The bottom of an old-fashioned washing machine lay rusting, upside down in the dirt.

He let the door slam behind him as he came swiftly out on the porch and down the three steps. The scent of Old Spice trailed into the car with him.

"Farrel—"

He pulled me close, his mouth finding mine. His kiss was hungry, as if he could never get enough, instantly making up for all the days he hadn't called.

At Maylene's, he went to the door for her. It was when they got back to the car that it all started.

"Sit in the middle, Farrel," she said. "Julie'll have a fit if she doesn't get to sit next to you."

His face stiffened.

I could have killed her.

"That's crazy," I sputtered.

"I want to sit by the window, anyway" she added.

On the road, she batted wide eyes at him and asked question after question, clearly designed to flatter his ego.

Once she looked over at me and said, "You're awfully quiet, Julie. You're not mad about something, are you?"

"Why would I be mad?" I demanded, my voice shrill and out of control.

At the college, we slipped past the monitor and up the steps to Farrel's room. His roommate, a dark-haired, good-looking guy with warm, brown eyes, looked up from his desk when we went into the room.

"You must be Julie," he said to me. "Farrel said you're a good-looking hunk o' woman."

My face burst into sunshine.

"She's Elvis Presley's girlfriend, you know," Maylene said through a pout and moved to scrutinize the prints of sports cars and half-naked women decorating the walls.

The corners of Farrel's mouth shot down.

The roommate's eyes popped. "No shit?"

"Elvis and I are only friends," I said, slipping my hand into Farrel's. He disentangled his fingers from mine.

"I need a word with Dave. You two go on to the car. I'll catch up with you."

We had lunch at the college deli, stopped by the record shop, then went to pick up my dress.

The sales lady suggested I try it on before she packaged it up for the trip home. I didn't really want Maylene and Farrel to have a preview of it, just in case I got to wear it tonight to the dance, but Maylene insisted I model it for her and Farrel.

When I stepped out of the dressing room, Maylene caught her breath. Farrel's eyes lit, and he let out a huge wolf-whistle.

"It's gorgeous," Maylene said, then abruptly turned away and went to examine some sweaters on a nearby rack.

I adored the dress. A glance in the mirror confirmed what I had hoped; it made me look elegant.

"Hurry up and get changed," Farrel said and tagged along behind her.

I tried to hurry, but I had to have help getting out of the dress, and it took the sales lady forever to wrap it up. As she finally handed the huge dress box over the counter to me, I happened to glance up toward the front of the store. Farrel and Maylene stood in the doorway, her face turned up toward his, and the afternoon glare backlighting their profiles into silhouettes. Even though they moved apart a few minutes later, the incident branded itself in my brain.

On the trip home, Farrel drove. Maylene crawled in back. When I saw she was asleep, I moved over to the hump seat close to him. Taking my hand, he brought my fingers to his lips and kissed each one.

When we dropped Maylene off, she scooted out of the car without looking at either of us.

"Thanks so much, you all, for letting me horn in," she said, and turning, she skipped up the walkway and waved. "See you later."

All the way to Farrel's, I prayed silently that he would ask me for a date to the dance, but he said nothing. Maybe he thought it was too late to ask.

By the time we got to his house and he still hadn't said a word about going anywhere that night, never mind to the dance, I summoned up my courage.

"Farrel, couldn't we go to the Christmas dance tonight?" I hated the timid tone of my voice. "I'm dying to show off my new dress. You wouldn't have to bother with a corsage. I don't like wearing them, anyway."

He shifted his eyes. "I can't tonight, Julie."

He stared out the windshield with glazed eyes as a young girl came onto the porch and yelled, "Pop needs you to help him set that water heater, Farrel."

"That's my youngest sister," he said.

"Do you have a card game tonight?" I asked, knowing full well that the guys he played poker with all had dates to the dance.

His silence went on for an eternity. "No, I don't have a card game. My old man's waiting, honey. I gotta go."

He opened the car door and got out as I slid over under the wheel. Two steps away from the car, he turned.

"Thanks for the ride to Magnolia. What do I owe you for gas?"

"Nothing. You don't owe me a damn thing."

He came back to the car window and, reaching his head inside, kissed my cheek.

"I'll call you. It's just that tonight . . ." He broke off and looked pained.

"I gave you everything I had to give last weekend, Farrel. I can't believe you haven't called since."

"Oh, come on, Julie. Don't be so serious about everything."

"How can I not be serious," my voice broke, "about what we did?"

"Farrel," called the sister, "Pop says get your butt in here, now!"

"In a minute!" he shouted back.

The girl went in and slammed the door behind her.

"I really have to go," he said. "I'll give you a call."

I put the car in gear and spun off so hard he had to step backward. When I looked in the rearview mirror, he was still standing in front of his house, watching me drive away.

At home, Mama's note said she'd ridden to her party with Mavis. I hadn't been inside the house five minutes when the phone rang. It was Maylene.

"Julie, I have something to tell you."

A sick foreboding crept over me.

"Farrel and I had a talk in the record shop. He complained that every time he takes you out he gets bombarded with folks asking if you're going steady."

I said nothing.

"I told him I understood completely because that was the way it was with Steve and me—constantly, 'Are y'all going steady?' Julie, what I'm trying to tell you is, Farrel asked me for a date to the Christmas dance tonight."

The memory of them standing in the doorway of the record shop reared up like a sea monster—mouth wide, fangs glinting.

"But I won't go if you're going to badmouth me all over town. I won't have it said that Maylene McCord stepped on the toes of her best friend."

"You won't have it said, but you'll damn sure do it, won't you?"

CHAPTER 33
Love Me

As I hung up the phone, all I could think of was: *Where did I get the guts to say that to Maylene?* Stupid me for believing she was my friend. More stupid me for believing I could make Farrel love me.

In a daze, I picked up a new record from the "commode" that had come in the mail from Elvis and put it on. How appropriate the title, "Love Me." The words set me to weeping and filled me with self-loathing as I realized they echoed exactly the message I had unwittingly given Farrel—that I would let myself be treated like a fool, just to be loved.

A knock came at the front door. I stole a peek through the living room window. It was Justin Moore, and he caught me peeping out. No way now could I pretend not to be home. No time to remedy my red eyes and swollen face. I flipped the switch and light pressed against the oncoming darkness of the December night.

His dark eyes searched mine when I opened the door.

"Are you all right?"

Even in the cold of the Christmas season, a lone moth found its way to bob around the hazy glow of the porch light. I shook my head.

"Not really." Fumbling for the handle, I pushed open the screen door. "I thought you were out of town."

"We got back early." He stepped inside. "I came by to ask if you will go with me to the dance."

I stared at him.

He rubbed his forehead. "I know it's late, but given what has happened."

"You know, then."

"I know. I was all excited to be home early. I called to tell Maylene we could go to the dance. I was going to ask her to go steady. Jesus! What happened today?"

"Betrayal."

Our eyes locked in mutual disbelief.

He clinched his fist. "It's monstrous."

"Your English class is reading *Medea*, right?" I said.

In a burst of laughter, we became two hurt friends, hugging each other. He pulled back. "Still, the word is right. It's monstrous."

The crisp scent of pine roping permeated the TAC House. Justin and I walked in a half-hour late. Every head turned to watch us. Everyone must know by now. With lifted chin, I steeled myself. Mama's broken-record admonitions against showing emotion in public finally made sense.

My evergreen velvet dress from Magnolia had a scooped neck and long sleeves that came to a point over the top of my hands. Justin had intended the circlet of red sweetheart roses for Maylene, but like a crown in my hair, it made me look like I really had descended from a royal house.

"Pull yourself together," my sensible voice counseled. "You sound as crazy as Mama."

The first couple I picked out in the crowd was Carmen. She had a date with a boy I didn't know. They sat at the table with Della, Faye, Rhonda, and Eugene.

The in-crowd filled a table close to the dance floor, except for two vacant chairs. Maylene and Farrel sat in the center, holding court. Maylene's dress, of red-and-purple changeable taffeta, was the one she and her mother had picked out weeks ago for this occasion. Mama loathed changeable taffeta. Said it was cheap and tacky. Maylene glanced at us, raised her eyebrows in surprise, and looked quickly away. Farrel downright gaped, obviously unable to believe Justin and I were together.

Darcy and Lynn got up and came straight over to us.

"What a bitch she is," Lynn said under her breath as she put an arm around my waist. "Her dress can't hold a candle to yours."

"No, yours is absolutely fantabulous," Darcy said, wobbling in her high-heeled spikes as she gave me a peck on the cheek. "I just can't believe she'd pull a stunt like this—betraying you, her best friend, and you, too, Justin. We'd bring you right over to sit at our table," she rolled her eyes, "but Maylene said we have to save those seats for Frances and Don. Where are they anyway, Lynn?"

"How would I know? We'd better get back to our dates. Y'all come over and talk to us later."

"Not a prayer," Justin said.

Lynn gave me an encouraging squeeze as she moved away. "Chin up."

Justin and I went to an empty table near the twenty-five foot Christmas tree, across the room from the in-crowd's table.

Like a glittering moon, a rotating ball of mirrored glass hung from the ceiling and sprayed fragments of light in circles around the dance floor.

"You look super," Justin said, pulling out a chair for me.

I forced myself not to steal another look at Maylene and Farrel.

Reading my mind, Justin said, "We'll choose just the right moment to make them face us."

That moment came sooner than I expected. The band, brought in as a special treat for the Christmas dance to replace the usual record-spinning DJ, launched into "Blue Christmas."

"I like that song," I said. "I should write Elvis to record it. I bet it would be a huge hit."

Carmen got up from her chair and started across the dance floor. Her strapless dress was black. Red ribbon trimmed the bodice. Like her dress for the Valentine dance, it was far too old for such a young girl.

"Look at her," Justin said. "Frisking like a hussy and on her way over here. Are you friends with her?"

"No."

"Hi, y'all," she said, approaching a chair across from us at the table. "Do you care if I join you for a few minutes?"

I shrugged. Justin stood.

"I'll get us some punch."

Carmen's eyes found mine as she slid into the chair.

"I saw them come in together—Maylene and Farrel. Are you okay?"

My heart twisted. "They betrayed me."

"At least now you know what kind of people they are."

"I was happier when I didn't know."

"The truth always hurts, according to my mother, but you'll get over it."

"You're wrong. I'll never get over this—betrayed by the person I believed was my best friend and with the man . . ." my voice broke, "I love."

"You will because he's a boy, not a man, and it's only a high school betrayal. Come to my house tomorrow, and I'll tell you about a betrayal you really might never get over."

"What are you talking about?"

Justin started across the room toward us.

Carmen shook her head. "Once again, wrong time, wrong place."

"I thought you were going to tell me how we're kin."

"I'll tell you that, too, while I'm at it."

Justin, balancing three cups of punch in his hands, managed a tight smile when he got back to the table. Ever the gentleman, he'd gotten a cup for Carmen, even though I knew he didn't want her to hang on with us. Taking two of them from him, I set one down in front of her.

She drained it in one swig and jumped right up.

"Come over to our table if you get bored. My date smuggled in a flask. We'll put some real punch into this Hawaiian tutti-frutti."

"Let's dance," Justin said when she was gone.

We moved as one with the music, swirling across the floor past Farrel and Maylene, whose lips were pressed tight.

"She doesn't like this," I said close to Justin's ear. "Us together, I mean, and really dancing, not like them—just standing close without moving their feet, like they're stuck in one place."

He laughed. "Serves her right. I'm going to turn so you can see him, too."

Farrel's typically glazed eyes flashed dark looks of anger toward us. My look back at him was equally dark, but with sad recognition that he cared so little for me he would come here with Maylene.

"Farrel has always said he couldn't dance," I told Justin. "I guess that's one thing he wasn't lying about."

We had only been back at our table a few minutes when the school principal, short-legged Mr. Younger, burst through the door and weaved his way through the dancing couples to the bandstand. Tugging on the bandleader's sleeve in the middle of a number, he whispered something to him, and the bandleader cut off the music in one swift motion. Mr. Younger moved to the mic, his head bowed.

"Boys and girls—"

The mic shrieked.

"I'll fix it," the bandleader said, stooping down to fiddle with a wire.

Mr. Younger bounced up and down on impatient toes and ran his fingers across the top of his balding head.

In a minute, the bandleader beckoned to him. "Try it now."

Through the babble of happy chatter, the principal spoke again.

"Boys and girls, please return to your tables. I have an announcement to make."

Skirts rustled, shoes scuffed, high heels clicked as kids sauntered to their seats. When the sounds of metal chairs scraping the floor had finally ceased, the Principal cleared his throat and moved his gaze from one table to another.

"This isn't easy for me to say, and it isn't going to be easy for you to hear, especially at a time like this—your Christmas dance."

He pulled a handkerchief from the breast pocket of his navy, pinstriped suit and blew his nose.

Uneasy whispers skittered through the crowd.

"Your friend and classmate, Frances Latimer, passed away at five p.m. this afternoon at Warner Brown Hospital."

Darcy's scream spiked the stunned silence. Lynn and Laura layered their arms around her shoulders in a comforting mantle. Bursts of weeping erupted. Justin stared at me with dilated eyes.

"Of what, Mr. Younger?" Maylene called out, her voice topping the hubbub.

Another hush fell.

"Influenza," Mr. Younger said.

I looked quickly at Justin.

"She has been out of school a few days, but I never dreamed it was that bad."

Knocking over chairs and shoving tables askew in their shocked state, kids navigated into huddles of the various cliques, girls' faces contorted with grief, and guys standing, hands jammed into pockets, looking as defiant and scared as they must have looked on some long-ago first day of school. Justin and I arose and approached the in-crowd.

Maylene reached out and, putting an arm around both of us, drew us in. With a face of shame, Farrel moved to the other side of Justin.

"I wondered why she and Don weren't here," Justin murmured, skillfully extricating himself from Maylene, who had leaned heavily against him. Instantly, she moved to Farrel, who looked over her shoulder at me with hollow eyes.

Unable to bear being so close to them, I pulled away and set off through the bedlam now reverberating from one side of the large dance hall to the other.

In the ladies' room, I stared at my reflection in the big mirrors behind the line of sinks. My cheeks were pale, and my eyes, like Farrel's, were large and hollow.

The door opened, and Carmen walked in. She, too, stared at our side-by-side lookalike reflections. Her eyes looked into mine in the mirror.

"I can't believe Frances is dead," I said. "It's unreal."

She continued to stare at me in the mirror. "I can't believe we look so much alike."

"You don't want to look like me. I'm so pale. I hope I'm not catching the same flu. She's in our carpool. She must have exposed us all."

I turned back to the mirror and pinched my cheeks to give them color.

"You aren't coming down with the flu," Carmen said. "The flu isn't even going around."

In the mirror, my eyes found hers again. "What do you mean?"

"Who else is in here?" she asked low.

"I don't think anyone is."

I watched her open and bang shut the doors on each of the eight stalls. The red-trimmed, scalloped ruffles on her skirt rustled as she swept back to me. We looked straight at each other.

"I have to say this fast," she said. "He may not know any better, but what Mr. Younger told everybody is not true—about the flu killing Frances. That's just the story her family is putting out. You remember my mother is a nurse?"

I frowned.

"Well, she's assigned to the floor Frances was on at the hospital."

She paused.

I shook my hands from the wrists.

"What? What?"

"She told me when she got home from work, before I left for the dance. Frances Latimer died of a botched abortion."

She put out a hand to steady me.

"Come to my house tomorrow. I'll tell you the truth about everything."

CHAPTER 34
Lawdy, Miss Clawdy

The next day after church, I dropped Mama off at Mavis's to play bridge.

"Pick me up at four," she said through the car window. "Where are you going?"

"I . . . just riding around."

"With Maylene?"

"Maybe. Bye."

I sped away, leaving her standing on the curb, frowning.

Heat rose up in my cheeks as I turned onto East Third Street and pulled up in front of six fourteen.

Peeling paint marred the siding of the small house. On the way up the cracked walk, I stepped on a gingko berry. Its dog poop smell reeked in my nostrils. Three concrete steps led up to a front stoop, barely big enough for two people to stand on. The doorbell dangled by a wire from off its mount. I reached to knock, but before I got my hand to the door, Carmen flung it open.

"Hello," she said. The stack of skinny, metal bracelets on her arm jangled as she tugged the bottom of her gold shirt down below the waistline of her black jeans. "So, no flu, huh?"

"No."

"Then you believe me? About Frances."

"I guess I do."

Her eyes registered sympathy.

"I didn't like Frances, but I know she was your friend, and I'm sorry about what happened."

I pulled my dark-green cardigan sweater together and fumbled with the buttons.

"Come in," she said.

"I stepped on a Gingko berry. I don't want to drag the smell inside."

"It doesn't matter. We step on them all the time. Mother slipped on one this morning going out for the paper and almost fell. It's cold out here. Besides, I think you'd better sit down to hear what I'm going to tell you."

Dead leaves swirled around the stoop. I didn't want to go inside her house. I rattled my keys, like Farrel did when he was impatient.

"I don't have time. Just say what you have to say."

"Okay, if that's how you want it." She stepped out on the stoop with me and closed the door behind her. "We're sisters."

I stared at her. "Who is?"

"Us, you and me. We're sisters."

The keys slipped from my hand and clanked on the concrete.

"Scott Morgan is my father, too. My real father."

Carmen stood tall, as if having triumphed in some contest between us that I never knew had taken place.

"You're saying that my father is your father?" I asked.

"Mother says so."

Anger flashed in me. "Just when did your mother divulge this information to you?"

"Ooo, *divulge*. Do you always use such big words?"

I couldn't resist. "Is divulge a big word?"

Her eyes turned hard. "She *divulged* it to me, sister of mine, when I showed her the picture of us at the dance. She said it was about time the truth was told."

"What about the dad you told us about—the military man?"

"He's only my stepfather, but I didn't know it that night."

"Has your mother let him in on this little fantasy?"

"He's always known. And it's not a fantasy. He and Mother married in time for me to be born on the right side of the blanket. I'm the one who was kept in the dark all these years."

The door opened a crack.

"Carmen, who is it?"

"Our long-awaited guest," Carmen said over her shoulder.

The door opened wider. The woman wore a white nurse's uniform and, once again, or still, the tacky silver earrings. A slight sneer touched her lips.

"We figured you'd show up one of these days. I knew who you were the minute I saw you at that concert at the stadium, but let's not discuss this on the doorstep for all the neighbors to hear."

She bent over, picked up my keys, and taking my arm, she steered me inside.

"You can call me Claudia. We don't stand on ceremony." She waved toward the couch. "Have a seat."

Two tattered easy chairs with sagging innersprings slouched opposite the TV. A sewing machine, splattered with spools of colorful thread and scraps of cloth, occupied a corner of the room. The house bulged with old lady clutter.

"When mother, Carmen's grandmother, got sick, she let the house go," Claudia said. "We need to keep our voices down." She gestured over her shoulder. "She's asleep in the back bedroom."

Silence pressed itself between us.

"Want a coke?" Carmen asked.

I shook my head.

"Carmen said she told you what really happened to Frances Latimer. Better keep it under your hat. Stupid kids, having sex in the backseat of a car and using no protection."

I shivered. "They were using the rhythm method."

She laughed. "That's not protection. Don't kid yourself. The only one hundred percent safe protection is the word 'no.'"

Carmen sighed.

"So don't be thinking you can get away with something." She tweaked Carmen's nose. "You're living proof you can't. Behave yourself, or I'll get you some lead britches."

My insides cramped with fear.

"Okay, Mother. I dig," Carmen said. "Now, tell her what you told me, about Scott Morgan being my father, too."

I couldn't believe I was sitting in this house, listening to what they were saying.

"I need to get going."

"Not yet you don't," Claudia said. "It's true. When I saw that picture of you two, I knew I couldn't keep a lid on it any longer. Listen, before I forget it in the heat of all this heavy stuff, Carmen told me about you and Elvis Presley. Says he sends you all his records. Does he?"

I drew my shoulders up tight against my neck.

"How can you bring up Elvis Presley at a time like this?"

"Good a time as any." She leaned toward me. "Ever send you 'Lawdy, Miss Clawdy'?"

I stared at her in disbelief.

"Named after me, I reckon," she said with a brassy laugh.

"Wait a minute. Wait a minute." I stuck out both hands. "Carmen and I are only a few months apart in age. There's no way this could be true."

"Come on, Julie. You're smarter than that," Claudia said, motioning to Carmen. "Sit over there next to her."

Carmen plopped down so close to me our shoulders touched. I squeezed against the sofa arm to disconnect.

Claudia pulled a cigarette lighter from her pocket and flipped it open.

"I never saw two kids who aren't twins look so much alike." With a flick of her thumb, she ignited a flame and lit a cigarette. Taking a deep drag, she exhaled smoke rings in my direction and smirked. "Ever see such good ones?"

I had, once, in the backseat of Farrel's car. Frances was dead from being pregnant and having it cut out of her. I might be pregnant, too. I wanted to run screaming out of this house, away from this scene, back into a past whose doors were forever shut to me now. One bad choice and my life could be ruined, or ended.

"I want you to know something about me, Julie. I never meant to harm your mother. I never would have knowingly fooled around with someone else's husband. Scott led me to believe he was single. By the time I learned he not only had a wife, but a pregnant one at that, I was pregnant, too."

"You were with him when my mother was . . . when . . . just before I was born?"

"The backseat of a car can be a mighty fine place, in a pinch."

"Mother!" Carmen exclaimed.

I pressed the heel of my hand to my forehead. *God help me.*

"She came here to find out the truth. I'm telling her." Claudia took another drag on her cigarette. She studied me, trying to read my mind, I knew, with eyes like smoldering, green pools behind her rolling smoke rings.

I could hardly breathe.

"There's no way you could have been living in this town and not known he was married," I said.

"We weren't in your mother's league, socially."

"Then how did you meet my . . . him?" I asked.

Claudia leaned back and laughed.

"He was hardly in her league, either. I met him down at the beer joint on South West."

Carmen took my hand.

"I always wanted a sister. When Mother told me about us, it was the best present I ever got."

Removing my hand from hers, I folded both of mine in my lap.

"Even if this outlandish story should happen to be true, I could never think of you as a sister."

"Why? You're an only, like me. Haven't you always wanted a sister?"

It was true. Throughout my lonely childhood, I had longed for someone to help me bear the consequences of my mother's broken life.

"Maybe I did, once, but I most assuredly don't want one now, especially not a *half* sister who came into existence like you did."

She shifted on the couch to study me. "I bet you don't want a father, either."

"I don't."

"You may not want him, but you need him," Claudia interjected. "You wouldn't be running all over town, making a fool of yourself over a guy who isn't right for you, if you had your dad."

Her words laid me bare. I crossed my arms over my breasts.

"Scott was irresponsible, no doubt about it," she went on. "But over the years, I've come to the conclusion that he was justified in looking for comfort outside his marriage. You see, Julie, some women are warm and loving and give their whole beings to their men. While others put a price tag on their high-falutin' selves and keep their men tied up in knots all their lives. That's why she lost him to me. She—"

"Mother!"

I leaped up. "I won't stay here and listen to this!"

I ran across the room and yanked open the door.

"You need to face reality, kid," Claudia called after me.

"Wait!" Carmen said. "Give me just five more minutes."

"To listen to more of your lies?"

She rushed over and grabbed my hand.

"It's not a lie. You and I are sisters."

I jerked my hand away. "I doubt that very much."

Claudia glowered at us.

"I gotta get to work. If you two are going outside, go. Don't stand there, half in and half out of the door, letting all that cold air in. And don't air this dirty laundry out there."

"And you, don't forget to take off your earrings," Carmen said, pulling the door shut behind us.

"One of your minutes is used up," I said over the fist in my throat.

A frigid wind swept between us. Standing there in the garish sunlight, I marveled that her cerulean-blue eyes were so like my own, and her face . . . almost an exact replica of mine.

"My stepfather—it seems so strange to call him that—has always been a great dad to me, but I want to know my real father. Go with me to see him. We could get to know him together."

"If your story should turn out to be true, I know him far too well already."

CHAPTER 35
The Sun, For Sorrow

That night at the dinner table, I pushed chicken a la king around on my plate with a fork in a futile effort to keep Mama from noticing that I couldn't eat. I wanted to confront her about the tale Carmen and her mother had told me, but I couldn't find the words.

She laid the back of her hand on my forehead.

"You're not coming down with that flu, are you? You don't feel hot."

"I'm just tired."

"I don't wonder—your little friend dying so suddenly and everything else."

"What else? Have you heard something?"

"Goodness, you're tense."

How could I be otherwise, knowing that right this minute I could be pregnant, never mind having just learned that my own mother may have been lying to me all these years about my father?

She leaned toward me.

"I only meant that, with the flu going around and Christmas just two days away, not to mention your having gone to the dance with that adorable Justin Moore . . ." She clapped her hands. "Why didn't you tell me you had a date with him?"

"Do I have to tell you everything?"

She bristled. "It might have been the polite thing to do, given that I got you that pretty new dress." She sighed and went on. "At least it

-174-

was money well spent. Justin Moore's a boy I totally approve of. Good family. Brought up right. Now you're showing some sense."

"We can't help who we love, Mama."

I braced myself for the pain it would renew in me to answer the inevitable next question: Who took Maylene to the dance? She knew Maylene dated Justin. But, oddly, she only looked at me with sad eyes and patted my hand.

"You've got to eat, otherwise, what'll I do with all this leftover casserole? Take it to the church tomorrow, I guess. A funeral on Christmas Eve. That's about as bad as it gets."

Before that night with Farrel, I'd never worried about being irregular. That night while Mama slept, her snores rattling down the hall, I lay tossing in my bed and counting the days over and over on my fingers. No matter which hand I started with, the result was always the same—an uncertain number which would simply have to be lived through one day at a time.

If I were pregnant, and Farrel refused to marry me, Mama would send me far away somewhere to a home for unwed mothers, where the baby would ultimately be put up for adoption. That's what had happened last year to a girl in the class ahead of us. The whole town would get wind of it, and I'd be disgraced forever. Or, if I could somehow find out how those things got done, I could take the chance that Frances took. If I survived, I would have to live with the guilt of killing my baby. No matter which, either shame or death stalked me.

I thought back to the night of Elvis's concert at the stadium, when I had so carelessly quipped to Della, Rhonda, and Faye that a nice girl might do IT for a Cadillac. I had done IT to win the love I so longed for, but what had I gained? Nothing but nauseating, unrelenting fear.

The yellow brick First Baptist Church took up an entire block two streets west of the square. Mama and I arrived a half-hour early in a downpour.

"I'm surprised there's such a crowd," Mama said, "what with flu going around. We'll be lucky to find a seat."

Mama took off her wide-brimmed black hat, held it under her coat, and we made a dash for it. The wind whipped our umbrellas inside out and ripped open my coat, letting rain splatter my navy wool dress.

Among Frances's many friends flooding into the church was a hoard of classmates who were not her friends, among them Della, Faye, and Rhonda with Eugene Hoffmeyer. Carmen, at least, had the grace to stay away.

Inside, Maylene busily orchestrated the saving of seats for the in-crowd. She beckoned us toward the middle section directly behind where she, Lynn, Laura, and Darcy sat, a short distance in back of the Latimer family. Mama and I squeezed in, and I found myself next to Miss Bolenbaugh. Maylene twisted around and reached for my hand over the back of her pew. I tolerated her finger-crushing grip for appearances, but kept my own fingers limp.

People streamed down the aisles on both sides. Ushers added more and more sprays to the bank of flowers down front beside the pulpit. The light in the church was dim for, on this misbegotten day, rain blurred the clear glass windows rising high above the sanctuary. Red and green candles and ribbons decorating the church for Christmas looked as incongruous as they would were it the Fourth of July.

Miss Bolenbaugh took the stubby pencil from its holder on the back of the pew, scribbled on a torn scrap of paper from her pocketbook, and slipped it to me. Squinting at the wobbly handwriting, I made out Shakespeare's words from the funeral scene in *Romeo and Juliet*: "The sun, for sorrow, will not show his head."

From the corner of my eye, I glimpsed Justin in a dark-blue suit and tie, sitting alone on the far left side of the church. He looked dazed, and the half-smile that touched his lips when he saw me quickly drooped.

My heart did its usual twisting flop when Farrel came down the aisle with a steadying hand on Don's shoulder. Both wore dark jackets, but Farrel had no tie. The two of them crowded into the pew unofficially reserved for extended family members, behind Mr. and Mrs. Latimer and the immediate family.

At the sight of the coffin being wheeled down the aisle, Mrs. Latimer, wild with grief, sprang from her seat and rushed to throw wide arms around the dark, polished box. Don and Mr. Latimer both stumbled across toes of people seated in their pews in a rush to get to her side, but when Don reached out, Mr. Latimer pushed him away. Weeping, Don allowed Farrel to assist him back to his seat.

Mama cringed. She never could bear a scene in public.

During the funeral, as I sat too numb to listen to the minister, everything I loved about Frances rolled across the screen of my mind, like a collage of scenes in a movie. The witty and clever remarks she spouted at exactly the right moment. Her perfect figure that flattered her clothes, instead of the clothes flattering her. Her contagious laugh that made us laugh, too. I would miss her.

The organist launched into "In the Sweet By-and-By," and we rose to file, row by row, past the open casket. Following Mama down the aisle, I repeatedly swallowed back the nausea flooding my mouth with saliva and hoped I wouldn't throw up. There was no way to escape this macabre viewing. Mr. and Mrs. Latimer's eyes were fixed on everyone. Besides, I could not betray to Mama, or to anyone, the slightest hint of my own agony.

When we approached his pew, Farrel looked over at me for the first time that day. His drawn face and fearful eyes mirrored my own. A reprimanding nudge from Mama broke our locked gaze.

Too soon we rounded the forward pew and approached the coffin. Death had rendered Frances unrecognizable. They had clothed her in the new gown she'd planned to wear to the Christmas dance. She had been so excited that afternoon, a lifetime ago, when she invited the carpool in after school to see the low-cut, red silk dress with spaghetti straps. In death, the red dress made her waxen face and limbs appear artificial against the white satin bedding of the casket.

"I can't wait to wear it," she had said.

Ominous words casually spoken, with no premonition that she would wear that dress forever.

I moved my hand to my abdomen. Looking down at the remains of my friend—once so vital and now so still—I prayed, but not for her. I beseeched the dear God in heaven not to let me be pregnant, too, and to help me get through the agonizing days until I found out.

By the time we arrived at the graveyard, the rain had slacked into a fine mist, sifting down on the headstones and vaults of El Dorado's dead.

"We don't need the umbrella," I said as we got out of the car.

"We do," Mama said. "It's the rain of fools. So light you don't realize it's coming down until you're soaked."

We squeezed into the tent with the crowd seeking shelter. Maylene maintained stoic posture throughout the service, while Darcy sobbed into a handkerchief. Laura clung to my hand, as if I could somehow give her strength, but I had none to give. It was all I could do to keep myself upright as my spike heels sank into the soggy grass.

Hanging on to Farrel's arm, Don moved carefully, like an arthritic in excruciating pain, to place a bouquet on the coffin. Maylene, Darcy, Lynn, Laura, and I—Frances's closest friends—each laid a white rose next to his red ones. The minister brought the service to a close by inviting us to a luncheon in the church's fellowship hall.

Sitting at the end of a long table with the in-crowd, I looked at them through my own dead eyes and wondered if they, like me, in the period of one short week, had lost their innocent perceptions of the world. I now knew that it was a serious place where one must be on guard, for some seemingly harmless choices could bring about consequences that would ruin one's life.

Still unable to force down a bite of food, I returned my tray to the kitchen and stepped outside to wait for Mama, now holding forth with Mavis and their other card-playing friends.

The rain had let up, but threatening clouds floated above. Pain in my back and legs from the constant tension caused me to move with as much care as Don as I went down the walkway, rounded the corner of the church, and stopped still. Farrel stood just ahead of me, smoking a cigarette. His pain-filled eyes sought mine.

"Hello, Julie."

"Hello, Farrel."

"I was hoping we'd get a chance to talk."

"Were you?"

"You seem surprised."

"You haven't called since the night we . . . Why would I think you'd want to talk to me now?"

He took a deep breath. "After that night, I got scared that things between us were getting too hot and heavy."

"You asked for all the hot and heavy. Remember, 'Don't tell me, show me'?"

He slumped. "Okay, okay."

"So you decided the best way to cool us down was to betray me with my best friend?"

"I didn't ask Maylene to the dance. She asked me."

"How convenient."

"It's true, Julie. When I saw you two girls at the Dairyette the night before, I knew you were trying to hustle up dates to the dance. I intended to take you."

I cut through the air with my hand.

"Just when did you plan on asking me? An hour before?"

His eyes flashed. "Isn't that when Justin asked you?"

"The fact is, you chose to take her instead of me."

"She asked me. I swear."

"You could have said no. You *would* have said no, if you . . ." I broke off.

"If I what?"

"Never mind. It's pointless."

"If I cared? Whether I admit it or not, Julie, I do. Listen, I have to know—did you come through like a champ?"

"Wasn't your protection a hundred percent safe?"

He shifted his eyes. "Yes. But a slip up could happen."

"Now you tell me."

"Please tell me, are you okay?"

"I don't know yet."

"Jesus!" He twisted sideways, like he'd been struck a blow. When he eased back upright, his voice was shaky. "When will you know?"

"Any day now. You don't have much time to work on your speech to convince everyone that you aren't the father."

He jerked, as if I had struck him.

"What do you think I am?" he asked hoarsely.

I could feel the cynicism in my smile.

"You would marry me, then?"

His face instantly turned skittish. He glanced over his shoulder.

"This whole Frances thing has knocked me for a loop."

"'This whole Frances thing'? Is that how you think of her death?"

"Give me a break. I don't want the same thing to happen to you. That's why I took Maylene to the dance."

"What do you mean, you don't want the *same* thing to happen to me?"

He avoided my eyes.

"You know, don't you, Farrel?"

He turned to go.

"I gotta look out for Don. He's pretty wrecked up."

I jerked his coat sleeve.

"You know the truth, don't you? I can see it on your face. Do you think you could manage to tell it, just this once?"

"I don't know what you mean."

"I mean, there isn't any flu. Never has been. And you know it!"

He sagged. "It's not supposed to get around. How did you find out?"

"Carmen told me."

"Carmen?" He looked stunned. "How on earth . . . ?"

"Her mother is a nurse. Assigned to Frances's floor at the hospital."

He pressed his fist to his forehead.

"God, I can't bear all this. It's my fault, you know."

"Your fault? But how?"

He took a shuddering breath. "I took them to get it."

"You took them to get the . . . ?"

"Don't say that word here." He looked over his shoulder. "That Sunday, the morning after you and me . . ." A single sob cracked his voice. He gritted his teeth and took a breath. "Don called me at six o'clock that Sunday and told me she was pregnant. He was frantic. They wanted to get rid of it but didn't know how. I took them that night to get it done."

"Where? Where did you take them? To a doctor in Little Rock?"

"It's against the law for a legitimate doctor to do a thing like that. We went to a back alley dump over in Texarkana." His voice broke again. "I could smell the house when the midwife opened the door. She put Frances on her dining room table and did it."

"How did you know about a place like that?"

He shrugged. "Some guys in the dorm were talking about it."

For a long time we stood there, silently looking at each other, then looking away. I fought the ache in my throat. He touched my sleeve with trembling fingers.

"I always knew you'd be special in my life."

I pulled away.

"Why did you take them to such a place?"

"I didn't have a choice. Don's my friend. He needed somebody to help him out of a jam and be with him so he could tend to her on the way back."

"Why didn't he marry her?"

Farrel thrust his palms upwards. "What would they have lived on?"

"Don's parents could have taken care of them until he got a job."

He poked at the grass with the toe of his shoe.

Nausea swept over me again.

"He paid for the abortion instead, didn't he?"

He looked pleadingly at me. "He's been accepted at Yale. A wife and baby would have ruined everything."

"And everything isn't ruined now?"

CHAPTER 36
Are You Lonesome Tonight?

While Mama fumbled in her purse for the car keys, Farrel helped Don into the blue Chrysler. I watched as they pulled out from the curb and drove away from the church. Unable to look away, I watched until the blinking rear signal light turned out of sight. Did some part of my essence linger in that car to remind Farrel of me? There would never be a day that I would not remember him.

The drive home, less than two miles, seemed to take forever. I still had a demon to confront—Mama.

At the house, she went to gather the mail while I went directly to my room, eased down on the bed, and closed my eyes, once again going over every detail of Carmen's fable that we were sisters.

I was born on June twenty-third. She was born the following November. That would make her five months younger than I was. Mama divorced my father before I was born, and I was positive she had never told me the truth about why. That was the one thing that made it impossible for me to rule out Carmen's story.

Claudia claimed she was having an affair with him at the same time Mama was pregnant with me.

"That would certainly be reason enough," I said, unaware that I was muttering out loud.

"Reason enough for what?"

I opened my eyes and jerked upright. Mama stood in the doorway of my room.

"Stop sneaking up on me."

"I didn't sneak. Reason enough for what?"

With an effort, I made myself get up and face her. The time had come.

"Mama, why did you leave my father? Tell me the truth."

"Not that again. For the umpteenth time, he was a ne'er-do-well."

She swept around and walked, with determined steps, toward the kitchen. I followed her, equally determined.

"This time, I won't let you cut me off."

She swept around to face me head-on.

"I'll tell you again, as I've told you before, he blew every dime my daddy left me. Don't you think that's enough of a reason?"

"You must have known all along he was blowing your money. And you were about to have me. Why did you pick that moment to get a divorce?"

"I didn't want to bring you into the world in circumstances like that."

Her face wore the familiar expression she put on when she was lying—eyes cut to the side, chin lifted. She wasn't a good liar.

"I don't understand," I pressed. "Divorcing him didn't change the circumstances I was born into. There was no money left for him to blow. There must have been some other 'circumstance.'"

"It's Christmas Eve. Let's not go at each other like this. Will you be all right if I go on to the party with Mavis tonight? Can you find something to do?"

I nodded, my throat swelling.

"We'll eat there. Shall I fix an egg salad sandwich for you?"

"No. I'm not hungry."

"You have to eat."

I moved in front of her.

"Mama, you have to tell me the truth."

"I've always told you the truth."

"I don't think so. Carmen says she is my sister."

Mama blanched. "You don't have a sister."

"Okay, a half sister. We share the same father, and her mother's name is Claudia. Does that mean anything to you?"

She laughed. "I know from you that she wears gaudy earrings."

"All right, if that's how you're going to play it. But be sure of this, I will find out, one way or another."

I turned to leave the kitchen.

"Just what are you insinuating?" she called after me.

I faced her. "If you won't tell me, I'll ask him."

"Him, who?"

"My father. Or maybe I should say Carmen's and my father, who told me, by the way, that he is going to serve you with a court summons for defying his rights to see me."

Mama clenched her fists. "That sorry son of a bitch!"

We stared across the room at each other.

"So you admit that Carmen's father is my father?"

"I've not admitted anything."

"You didn't deny it."

Her face twitched. "Just when did you go behind my back and see him, pray tell?"

"I didn't go behind your back. He came here."

"To this house? I'll slap a restraining order on him."

"It's true, isn't it, Mama? He is Carmen's father, too."

"God help me."

Bent and pressing her hands against her torso, Mama made her way to a chair at the breakfast room table and sat, weeping.

"Don't cry, Mama," I said, sitting next to her.

"I so hoped you wouldn't find out," she said, patting her face to stem the tears.

I fished in my pocket for the lace-edged handkerchief I had been strong enough not to use at the funeral and handed it to her.

"How could I not have found out? She looks so much like me."

"She does, but she can't," Mama sobbed into the already damp cloth. "I want you to be free from that sordid part of our lives. All these years, I've protected you, and now this."

"Tell me what happened."

She drew a long, shuddering breath.

"A few days before you saw them at that Elvis concert, Mavis told me that Claudia was back in town and had brought a daughter your age with her." Mama got up and walked slowly to the row of windows in the den. "It's raining again. Sometimes I wish we lived in the north where it snows in December, instead of all this infernal rain."

I thought of Frances in the polished box out in the cemetery. Was rain seeping into her casket, ruining the red dress? And could the cold chill her more than she was already chilled?

My own voice broke when I urged, "Go on with the story, Mama, please."

She turned to face me.

"One day, on my way home from a doctor's appointment when I was pregnant with you, I stopped by your father's store to surprise him. It was raining that day, too."

I sat up straight.

"He had his own business?"

"Yes, a dry goods store on Jefferson. It cost more money to keep it open than it brought in. He wasn't a good business man."

"Go on. What happened?"

Her face crumpled, but she fought back, straightening her shoulders.

"The lights were on, but the door was locked—in the middle of the afternoon. Something was wrong. All I could think of was that a robber had tied him up in the back of the store. I had a key so, as quietly as I could, I went inside."

Mama wrapped her arms around herself.

"There was no one in sight on the sales floor. He only had one clerk left on the payroll by then. He must have given her the afternoon off. I knew he kept a small revolver behind the counter. I slipped off my shoes and tiptoed to get it. The floor creaked with every step I took, but I made my way to the curtain that closed off the back room and yanked it open. They were there, together—him and Claudia—on a little single bed he kept there for just such opportunities, I surmised."

I sat still, staring at her. "You don't mean . . . ?"

"Yes, that is exactly what I mean. *In flagrante delicto*. I should have shot him. The whole town knew before I did that he was . . . involved with her. So humiliating."

She came back to the table and, sitting, clutched my hand.

"The worst part was, the shock was so great I almost lost you. I was in the hospital for a week. Every day your father came, begging me to forgive him, but by then I'd found out that the other woman—this Claudia of the dangling earrings—was pregnant, too."

Mama wiped her eyes on the soaked hanky.

"The day I got out of the hospital, I called a locksmith and had every lock on the house changed. The next day, I filed for divorce. I vowed he would never hurt you, and I've dedicated my life seeing to it that he does not."

"By keeping me away from him?"

She turned surprised eyes on me.

"Can you think of any better way? I had a friend who was a judge. He personally fixed it so your father did not get visitation rights for years."

"Well, now *he* has a friend who is a judge. Shame on you, Mama. Shame on you both."

"I did it for our protection. He's a violent, wild man. Not to mention a drunk."

"I've only seen him violent once."

"Have you ever seen him sober?"

I thought back to the night he stood on our porch during my party, while bugs bobbed around his head beneath the porch light that Elvis so correctly had said needed a yellow bug light.

"Once."

She wrung her hands.

"Can't you take my word for it?"

"If he's so bad, why did you marry him in the first place?"

Her face reflected heartbreak of the sort I harbored inside myself about Farrel.

"I thought I loved him."

"Did it ever occur to you that maybe I needed my father all those years?"

She blinked. "Needed? Why in God's name would you have needed him?"

"According to Claudia, I needed him, and still do, to keep me from making a fool of myself over a guy who isn't right for me."

Unobtrusively, so not to attract her attention, I edged my hand over to rest on my abdomen. "And maybe I do."

"*I've* told you Mr. Budrow isn't right for you. That woman isn't giving you any news. For the love of God. You think he could have met your needs better than I have, working my fingers to the bone to feed and clothe you all your life?"

"Okay, okay, he screwed up, but I'm not sure he deserved what you did to him to get even."

"Is that all you have to say? 'Okay, he screwed up'?" She shook her head, despair written on her face. "I suppose you'll have to find out for yourself what kind of person he is. And when you do, don't come crying to me that, just when you thought you could trust him, he jerked the rug out from under you, betrayed you, and made you look like a fool. Because he will. He's a master at that game."

As stiffly as though she were a woman twice her age, Mama got up from the table and went back into the kitchen. She pulled a sauce pan from the cabinet beneath the counter and took eggs from the Frigidaire.

"I saw you talking to Mr. Budrow, by the way, outside the church during the luncheon."

"Did you?" I asked dully.

"What did he have to say about your going to the dance with Justin? For that matter, what about Maylene? I don't suppose she was happy about it."

"She was happy enough. She went to the dance with Farrel."

"I told you so." Mama filled the saucepan with water at the sink and, turning in my direction, began carefully placing the eggs into it, one at a time. "And what did he have to say for himself today?"

"He said he drove Don and Frances to get the abortion that took her life."

"Abortion?" Mama's face paled.

"Yes. There isn't any flu."

"How did you find out?"

"My sister told me."

Mama shook her head.

"Look at it this way. At least, for once, you got the news before Mavis."

"He drove them? But why would he be discussing such a thing with you?"

"Because I might be pregnant, too."

The pan clattered out of her hand, splashing water and breaking eggs all over the floor. Mama stood absolutely still while yolks and gelatinous egg whites oozed across the linoleum.

I got up and went to a drawer and pulled out several dishtowels.

"How could you do this to me?" she said, her face crinkling again.

"I didn't do it to you. I did it to make Farrel love me."

A long silence ensued while our eyes locked in a fragment of understanding across the sticky mess on the floor.

"I'll have to send you to Dallas, if you are," she said, her hands trembling.

I gave her a wry smile.

"I don't think a girls' school would take a pregnant student."

"Not a girls' school, a home for unwed mothers."

I lifted my chin.

"No, you'll not be sending me anywhere, pregnant or not. If I am, I will stay right here and have the baby."

"Your life will be ruined if people find out, and so will mine. Surely, after what happened to Frances Latimer, he would marry you."

"He might, but he wouldn't be happy."

I knelt down to wipe the floor.

Carefully, as if she might break, Mama got down on her hands and knees beside me.

"Let me help you, honey. It's my mess. I went to your room . . . what seems like a century ago now, to tell you something came in the mail. From Elvis. It's on the—"

"I know. The commode."

Mama and I looked at each other for a long moment, then shared a half-smile.

CHAPTER 37
WHEN MY BLUE MOON TURNS TO GOLD AGAIN

It was late afternoon when Mavis honked in the driveway. Old folks' parties began early but usually went on until after midnight, especially at Christmas. I stood at the front door, watching, as Mama flounced across the damp lawn in her spike heels, dyed to match her red party dress, which brought back the sight of Frances lying in her coffin. A person would never have thought Mama had watched the burial of my friend that very day, nor heard the news that she might soon be a grandmother.

The light went on inside the car when she opened the passenger door, allowing me to witness her arm waving as she spouted something to Mavis. Then Mavis's head turned to focus toward the house, trying to get a glimpse of me in the doorway, no doubt. I stepped back and shut the door. Mama wouldn't miss getting the jump on her about what really killed Frances, but I knew she would conceal the fact that I might be pregnant for as long as it was humanly possible.

Turning, I noticed the package from Elvis lying on the commode. I tore it open and removed a new forty-five and a note. When he had first begun writing me, he had written on pretty greeting cards. Then it had changed to his stationary. This missive looked to have been hastily scratched out on a torn sheet from a lined tablet.

Dear Juliet,
Thinking of you this afternoon, my good luck charm. I'm doing recording sessions in New York. There's a lot of pressure in this business, and

sometimes I feel like it's all coming down right on my head. I'm sending another record for you. If the words in the title come true for me, it'll be because I have a little free time to get away from it all and be back with my friends again in the beautiful southland—"When My Blue Moon Turns To Gold Again."
Still remembering,
Elvis

The music made me hurt so much inside I had to shut it off. In the den, I flopped down in Mama's easy chair. It brought me no comfort. I stared at the blinking lights on the Christmas tree, counting on my fingers, yet again. In spite of my brave talk to Mama, I was scared of being pregnant. I didn't want to be. Not yet. I wanted to be free to maybe go to college and do something with my life.

I thought back on the things Farrel had said as we talked after the funeral. He was so hopelessly lost from me now that it was hard to fathom that we had ever been close enough to make love. He had never shared with me his hopes or his dreams, and few of his likes and dislikes, but the thought that I would never again lay my head on his chest and hear the beating of his heart wrenched my own.

The ringing of the phone broke the silence.

"Julie, it's Maylene."

"I know."

She half laughed. "Yes, I guess you know my voice by now. Listen, I thought our crowd should be together tonight, because of Frances, you know, and not be alone, so if you want to come over, I'd like you to be with us. Do you think you can get the car?"

"Yes, I can get the car."

"Well, come on over."

I pictured walking in her door and seeing the crowd, huddled together and repeating their expressions of grief, which this afternoon seemed exaggerated to the point of being fake, instead of expressing true, inner pain. I could imagine myself in her living room, standing apart from the others, unable to feel connected, even when they drew me into their circle. Her betrayal had permanently severed our friendship, leaving only a ragged edge of hurt and disbelief in me. Although we would run into each other all the time at school, I knew that Frances's death had cut the invisible cord that bound me to the in-crowd and had set me adrift, to find my own way.

Oddly, I wasn't scared of that, and what was even weirder, I knew I no longer needed Maylene or the others of the in-crowd to make me an acceptable person. I was what I was, and running with them could not make me better or worse. The most mind-blowing thought was that going with Farrel wouldn't make me any prettier or more attractive either. For some reason that I couldn't for the life of me figure out, that idea made me feel like maybe I could act around him like a person the age I was, instead of being like some needy, inferior being, begging for his love.

"Well, are you coming?" Maylene's impatient voice demanded. "Or are you still mad at me for going to the dance with Farrel?"

"No, I'm not mad at you, Maylene. You did what you had to do. And so did he. But no, I won't be coming tonight."

I hung up the phone and watched darkness creep up to the windows. I had done what I needed to do with Maylene, but still I had no peace. I had been wrong about everybody—Maylene, Farrel, even Mama. If I couldn't trust my perceptions about people, how could I ever know who anyone really was? Or maybe I had closed my eyes to all the signs they had given me because I didn't want to see them as they truly were.

Anyway, it didn't matter anymore. Frances was gone and could never be brought back. Maylene had shown her true colors. And Mama had lied to me all along, just get even with my father. Even though I could see why she would feel the need to strike back at him, she at least owed me the right to have a relationship with him.

The house had never been so silent. I had never been so alone. I wandered to the front door to turn on the porch light for Mama. When I flipped the switch, Elvis's words, spoken that night when he walked me to the door, came back to me. Maybe that was what I had to do tonight.

Once again, it was a warm night for December. I pulled into the gravel driveway of the little house that, like Farrel's, was also on the wrong side of the tracks.

My father was stringing Christmas lights on a plump pine tree in the front yard. His face changed from astonished to quizzical as he approached the car.

I rolled down the window and sat, looking at him.

"Julie?" he asked.

"Yes."

"I'm glad to see you," he said, looking into my eyes, "but what finally brings you to me?"

"I need you . . . to help me put up a yellow bug light."

CHAPTER 38
PLAYING FOR KEEPS

My father gave me a strange look and, after a moment, opened the car door for me.

"There may be a spare bug light inside on the pantry shelf, but why . . . ?" He broke off, shaking his head in a manner that conveyed his hopelessness of ever getting an answer. "I am just now putting up the Christmas lights," he said, "on Christmas Eve, but like they say, better late . . . " His voice trailed off.

"Let me help."

He tilted his head and smiled, his eyes reflecting surprise. He seemed sober, and no trace of alcohol marred his breath.

"Your mamaw and papaw aren't here. They'll be sick to miss you. They're always asking when they're going to see you again. They're just up at the church supper. Maybe they'll get home before you leave." He looked away. "I don't go to church much anymore, but you can see by all the Christmas decorations, I'm not a heathen, yet."

I followed him to the tree.

"So how's your job? Working on an oil rig, isn't it?"

He looked determined.

"Going great, and I plan to keep it that way. Bring that end of the lights around here."

We worked in silence for a while, and then he asked, "How are you getting along since your friend died in such a terrible way?"

It was my turn to be astonished.

"How did you know about that?"

"I have coffee downtown every morning with some hunting and fishing buddies."

"You found out from *them* about Frances Latimer's botched abortion?"

He raised his eyebrows. "At least you don't beat around the bush, like your mother. How did you ever become so outspoken, living with Elizabeth?"

"You answer my question first."

"It's a small town."

"Not good enough," I said.

He nodded. "One of my buddies was a relative. He let it slip. When I heard, I swamped heaven with prayers, thanking God it wasn't you."

"You did?"

"Of course."

We stood, looking into each other's eyes. Finally I said, "But you hardly know me."

"I may not know everything there is to know about you, but you're my daughter, and I . . . you know. Even if I haven't been much of a father to you, you know, I . . . you know."

No, I didn't know. Still, his words sent an unfamiliar warmth surging through me—a gladness I'd never experienced.

He lifted another string of lights from the battered cardboard box on the ground, and together we worked to untangle it.

"I thought maybe *she* told you about Frances," I said. "She told me."

He looked sharply at me. "Who?"

"You know who I mean. Please, be the one man alive who will play it straight with me."

He slumped.

"I suppose I knew you'd find out about her, sooner or later."

"How could I not? She looks exactly like me. It's true, then? She's really my sister?"

"What did your mother say?"

"She told me everything."

"Everything?"

"Everything."

Cutting his eyes away, he clipped the last light to a lower branch.

"Well, that clears that up. It's just that I doubt very seriously if she told you the *whole* truth."

"What's that supposed to mean?"

He scoffed. "Well, didn't you come here to get me to shine a bug light on the subject?"

We exchanged an awkward smile.

"I would listen to your side, yes," I said.

He opened his mouth to speak. I waited. He shook his head.

"Nothing. Forget it. Someday, maybe, but not now. It's Christmas. It's such a beautiful night. You want to just sit out here?" He pointed to a curved, concrete bench near the decorated tree. "The outdoor chairs are put up for the winter. I'll go turn the lights for the tree on."

"Before you do, a favor?"

"Anything for you," he said and hesitated. "Well, almost anything."

"Ask your friends to keep it under their hats about Frances. I would hate to see it get all over town and bring more shame on her memory."

"Men don't spread gossip like women do."

He went inside, and a few minutes later, the colored lights on the tree blazed into the darkness. He returned, carrying a portable radio and a bug light, which he handed to me.

"Here it is, for what it's worth." He flipped on the radio, and Bing Crosby singing "White Christmas" rang out into the night. "The tree is pretty, but more so because you helped me decorate it."

Sitting beside me, he looked at my hand, like he wanted to hold it, but he didn't.

"I really do need the light bulb. Elvis said it would get rid of bugs."

"I saw his show down at the stadium last year. So he's your boyfriend, huh?"

"Where did you hear that?"

He gave a cynical laugh. "Like I said, it's a small town."

"The gossip circuit doesn't always get it right. He's not my boyfriend, but he is my friend."

"Then he's not the guy who hasn't played straight with you," he said, looking directly at me.

I only shook my head. I knew I'd break down if I tried to answer, and I had not come here to cry on his shoulder.

"I won't try to convince you that it's a good thing you found out what he was like before it was too late," he said, "but it is."

If it's not too late already.

He seemed to read my mind.

"It's not, is it? Too late?"

"I don't think so," I managed to say.

His breath of relief caught itself up short as he saw my face, naked with truth.

"Do you want to talk about it?" he asked.

I couldn't bring myself to tell him I might be pregnant. It was just more than I could handle with a man I hardly knew, even if he was my father. I shrugged and told only half the truth.

"Just that he and the girl I thought was my best friend went to the Christmas dance together. Lost them both in one fell swoop."

"Betrayal," he said. "The sin of the angels."

"That sin was ambition."

"They are one and the same."

This time he allowed himself to gently pat my hand resting on the bench between us.

"You're acquainted with betrayal, then?" I asked. "I thought you were the one who did all the betraying."

"I didn't see it that way. I bet your friends don't see it that way, either. No doubt they feel fully justified in their actions, and they would say it was your behavior that made them do it. In this life, it all depends on whose ox is being gored."

"Is that how it was with you and Mama?"

"Absolutely. For years it was all her fault, in my mind."

"What is the truth?" I asked. "My quest is to find the truth."

"That could take some time," he said, "and we decided not to pursue that tonight. Just don't take it out on Carmen. You're both victims. I hope you girls will find some comfort in each other someday."

Neither of us knew where to look.

My father shrugged. "One truth is, this night is beautiful."

"Playing for Keeps" came on the radio, and Elvis's voice floated around us.

"Nobody can tell you when you can and can't dance," my father said. "Would you do me the honor?"

Surprised and pleased, I walked with him to the open area in front of the house. He moved smoothly, even when the dead grass tried to trip us up. He was humming along with Elvis when he sneaked a peek at his wrist watch. I wanted him to know I'd caught him in the act.

"Do you have to be somewhere?"

He stopped dancing and broke away.

"Yeah, there's a party down at the saloon tonight. I told the gang I'd drop by. You know, have a toddy and sing a few Christmas songs."

"Like 'Silent Night'?"

He chuckled. "No, more like 'I Saw Mommy Kissing Santa Claus.'"

"Okay."

I walked toward the car.

"Hey, why don't you come with me?"

"To a party at a saloon?" I asked, incredulous.

He looked off to one side.

"Yeah, well, maybe that isn't such a great idea. But listen, Chicken Little." He took quick breaths. "Mom and Pop'll be home pretty soon. Why don't you hang around and surprise them. Be here to wish them a Merry Christmas? Sit there on the bench, or come inside. I'll turn the lights on in the living room for you."

"Some other time," I said, opening the car door.

"I'm so glad you came, honey," he said, unable to hide the relief on his face that I was going. "Have a Merry Christmas, and come back again, soon. Will you?"

"I'll try."

"Promise me you will. There won't be a party next time. We'll have more time together then."

"Sure," I replied, turning the key in the ignition and shifting into reverse. "We'll have more time then."

CHAPTER 39
I'll Remember You

The in-crowd begged me to celebrate New Year's Eve with them.

"We're going to the dance tonight at the country club," Laura said when they stopped by the house that afternoon, ready to chain me up and drag me there, if necessary.

I hadn't seen any of them since Frances's funeral.

"Somehow, I don't feel like celebrating," I said, following them into the kitchen.

"We can't mourn Frances forever," Maylene said, helping herself to a slice of coconut cake Mama had left on the counter.

"Oh right," I said. "It's been a whole week."

Maylene shot me a dark look. Laura clucked her tongue.

"It won't be the same if you aren't there," Lynn said. "Cut me a piece, too, Maylene."

"And me." Darcy opened the silverware drawer and took out some forks. "I'm going to wear the same thing I wore to the Christmas dance. You could wear that sensational green number of yours again."

I sat at the table and indicated that they should join me.

"I don't have a date."

"I've got the answer to that," Lynn said. "My cousin from Boston is here. The Mayflower Mister, I call him, because he's always bragging that he can trace his lineage all the way back to the Mayflower. As if we weren't kin."

"He should fit right in at the club," I said.

"Seriously, Julie," Maylene said, licking a blob of white icing off her lip, "you have to go with us. We're doing it in memory of Frances, and she'd want you to be there."

We're going out to a party in memory of Frances, while she is lying in the grave, and in her party dress, no less. All I said was, "I can't go without a date."

"Eugene broke up with Rhonda," Darcy said, twirling an imaginary mustache."

"Don't do that." I swiped at her hand.

She turned a startled face to me. "Why, in heaven's name?"

"Frances always did that when she was planning mischief. It was her trademark gesture."

Darcy's face turned serious.

"Julie, you've got to snap out of it. You're taking Frances's death too hard. I'm worried about you."

"How can you take someone's death too hard? She's gone, forever. Not going to come back tonight at the dance wearing her pretty red dress they buried her in."

Maylene took hold of my wrist.

"Julie, you sound like you've gone off the deep end."

When I thought about the fact that I might be pregnant, too, I felt like I might go mad. They didn't know about that. I caught myself up short. They didn't know the true cause of Frances's death, either. They still thought she'd died of the flu.

Mama's keys rattled in the back door. I knew I had to cool it. I didn't want her thinking I'd flipped my lid.

Leaning heavily on the table with one hand, she gave me a peck on the forehead.

"Got off early today."

"The cake tastes so fresh, like the coconut came right off the boat from Hawaii, Mrs. Morgan," Laura said.

Mama's weary face revived.

"Enjoy it, girls. I'm heading for the shower."

When she was gone, Maylene took me by the hand. I kept my own hand limp in her grasp.

"Listen, Julie, would you be willing to go to the dance with Don?"
My mind shattered.

"Don would show his face at a dance with Frances dead only a week?"

"I told you. We're paying tribute to Frances by doing this," Maylene said. "He's part of it. She'd have wanted us to. Don hasn't come down with the flu yet, so you can't catch anything," she continued. "And they're going ahead with the dance, so no one must be very worried about flu."

"I'll have to think about it," I said.

"No, you need to make up your mind right now. The dance starts in," she looked at her watch, "seven hours. We have to know who's coming so we can get a table big enough."

I looked straight at her. "Who are you going with?"

"Not Farrel, if that's what you're asking. And not Justin. Steve is the best dancer I've ever gone out with. He asked me, and I accepted. So there. Will you go with Don?"

"No. I'll go with Lynn and her cousin. Tell Don I said, 'Assume a virtue, if you have it not.'"

Maylene rolled her eyes. "Deep end, for sure."

I did wear my green dress. I wondered if Justin would remember it. Nobody seemed to know whether he was even coming to the dance.

Lynn's Mayflower Mister came to the door for me at eight thirty. He was "drop dead" gorgeous—too good-looking for an all-American boy. After he deposited me in the backseat and went around to the driver's side, Lynn whispered over the seat to me.

"He goes to an all-boys school back in Boston and doesn't know as much about girls and dating as boys around here do."

"Lynn, are you sure you want me to drive?" he asked, sliding in.

"It's your big chance. Don't worry. It's pretty much a straight shot from here." She turned to me. "He doesn't get to drive very often up there. Too much traffic. Right?"

"Right," he said.

The country club glowed with the lights from its chandeliers. A live band played at just the right volume, so we could feel the music and hear ourselves think at the same time.

Our table was a big round one that could seat all nine of us—the five carpool girls and the four dates. I felt like I had returned to Dilbertsville, sharing the Mayflower Mister with Lynn, but no one paid me much attention.

Every year, young people from all over the state came to the El Dorado Golf and Country Club for what was known as "the best New Year's Eve dance in Arkansas." The club bulged with people, garlanded in holiday finery and humming around each other like bees in a hive. So many hovered around tables and bumped elbows on the dance floor that it was impossible to tell who was there that we might know.

Like a beaming apparition, Eugene Hoffmeyer appeared at our table midway through the evening and lived up to my unvoiced predictions by asking me to dance. Much as I dreaded it, I accepted. So far, absolutely no one else had approached me, except the Mayflower Mister, who didn't know one foot from the other.

"We'd be going steady, and you wouldn't be a wallflower, if you'd been a little nicer to me," Eugene said as I struggled to move my toes fast enough to dodge his flapping feet.

"What an unfortunate mistake on my part," I replied.

He bloated with self-satisfaction, totally missing my sarcasm.

"Why isn't Rhonda with you tonight?" I asked.

His face drooped. "We split the sheet."

"Not a very polite way to put it," I said.

"Just a wishful way. I wish we had shared a sheet."

"Please, spare me."

"By the way, your current flame is here tonight, if you hadn't noticed."

I stared at Eugene. "Who do you mean?"

He laughed. "Got so many, huh? Old Farrel. Right over there with the same beer-slushing cronies he always hangs out with. He's been staring at you all night. He could at least ask you to dance, like I did, especially since you're . . ." He broke off.

"What? A fifth wheel?" Only, in my case, it was a ninth.

He smirked. "You said it. I didn't."

As Eugene slowly turned me on the dance floor, I allowed my eyes to pass across the dimly lit corner where Farrel sat next to Don. He stared up at me with a look that threatened to strip away all my resolve to put him out of my mind. Our gazes locked until Eugene turned me again and the band came back into view. Steeling myself against looking toward that darkened corner again, I willed myself to endure the remainder of the dance, which I vowed was my last ever with Eugene Hoffmeyer.

On the way back to the table, someone snatched me from behind, away from Eugene's guiding hand on the small of my back, and propelled me out through the French doors and down the steps to the golf course. I knew who it was.

The night was cold and the stars, brilliant. I turned and looked into Farrel's face. An instant later, we slammed into each other's arms. He kissed me again and again—my lips, my cheeks, my eyes—and I returned his kisses with my own, filled with longing, starvation, and the indisputable knowledge that, no matter where our diverse paths would lead, some part of us would always belong to each other.

His fingers slipping down into the top of my dress jarred me to my senses.

"What in the name of God am I doing?" I murmured, breaking away from him and half running across the green.

"Give me a minute, Julie," he said, stumbling after me. He seized my arm. "I need to talk to you, and grabbing you like this was the only way I could think of to do it."

"I'm cold."

"I'll get your coat."

"I won't be out here long enough." I writhed in his grip, but he held me tight.

"Just hear me out."

When I stopped trying to pull away from him, he slipped out of his suit coat and put it over my shoulders. All the other guys wore dinner jackets. An unfamiliar feeling of pity for him arose in me. He wouldn't know what to wear to a place like this. Don should have told him.

The scent of Old Spice lingering in his coat assailed my senses, reviving the low, familiar ache he always stirred in me. He peered into my face.

"Are you?"

"As I said at the church last week, isn't it a bit late to be asking me that?"

"I'm nearly crazy, worrying about it. I've called, but your mother always answers the phone. I left messages with her. Did you get them?"

I nodded.

"So you just didn't want to call me back?" He turned his eyes away, out into the darkness. For a while, we were silent. "So answer me. Are you?"

"I still don't know yet."

What I did know was that I wouldn't tell him, if I were.

"Please let me know when you find out. I don't think you could be. I was careful."

I said nothing.

"So what's happened to you?" he demanded. "It seems like you've just dropped out. You haven't been around. It's like you went into the locker room and never came out again."

"Don't exaggerate. It's only been a week since I saw you and everybody else at Frances's funeral."

Again silence, while I called up my courage.

"I owe you an apology, Farrel."

His brow knitted. "What for?"

"I chased you—when I should have been cleaning up the mess in my own family."

"I don't follow."

"I went to see my father the other night. I think I wanted you to solve some problems that I should be working out with him. At least that's what Carmen says."

"Carmen?"

"My 'twin.'"

Recognition dawned on his face.

"Oh yeah, your 'twin.' Well, listen, you don't owe me any apologies. Let's start over. No girl has ever made me feel the way you did—and still do. We light fires together. You know we do."

I simply looked at him in the starlit darkness. He was dismissing something that had taken all the courage I could drag up to say.

"Is that silence a yes or a no?"

He wanted my body. His hopes were pinned on my not being pregnant—and so were mine. And yet, if I weren't, he wouldn't hesitate to put me right back into waiting, wondering. Was I or wasn't I?

"Don't say no, Julie."

"Now you're the one saying 'don't.' Here's your jacket back."

"Wait. Don't go yet. Look at all the stars out tonight. Don't you wonder what's out there?"

"I wonder that all the time."

He took my hands.

"Wish on a star with me."

He closed his eyes and squeezed his forehead into wrinkles, wishing hard. I made my own wish quickly, while memories flooded back to me of those first, bright days of Elvis. The concert where I first saw him. The pink Cadillac. The excitement that rocked me every time a letter or a record came from him. The wonderful, glorious fun of being part of the in-crowd. And the unforgettable times with the guy standing here, pressing my fingers to his lips.

Music floated faintly out to us from inside.

He tilted his head.

"That song, it seems familiar."

"Elvis recorded it back in June," I said, withdrawing my hands from his. "It's called, 'Any Way You Want Me.'"

"That's me," he said. "I'll be any way you want me."

If only that were true. I turned away.

His voice stopped me.

"I'm just a good ole boy and I can't really help myself. You shouldn't be so hard on me."

"I can't really help *myself*," I said. "But, Farrel, you're not *just* a good ole boy. You're a lot more than that."

"Does that mean you'll think about it?"

I moved away.

"Are you sure you want to leave us with nothing but regrets?" he called out as I walked through the damp grass back toward the club house. "At least promise me you'll remember, 'cause whatever happens, I'll remember you. I'll remember you, Julie."

His voice faded into the noise of the crowd as I went inside and shut the door behind me. His words were still with me even when the clock struck twelve and the band played "Auld Lang Syne." They stayed with me when the party ended and we returned to our homes.

In my bed, in the last darkness left before dawn, his words and the sound of his voice still echoed in my mind.

"I'll remember you."

Sunlight streaming through the window woke me. For a moment I was myself again, the girl I had been before Farrel, before the in-crowd, before the terrible loss of Frances. I got out of bed and padded to the window. The gloom of the old year seemed to have been washed clean and replaced by a dazzling blue sky of hope. Several minutes passed before the omnipresent fear punctured my serene state to remind me—I was still awaiting my "friend."

THE END

BUT WAIT—THERE'S MORE!

Don't Miss Book II
in The Days of Elvis Series!

In Those Dazzling Days of Elvis

by Josephine Rascoe Keenan

A secret rules her life.

In the days when Elvis Presley dazzled the nation, his "good luck charm," Julie Morgan, a small town girl bound by the social code of the 1950s, makes a serious mistake in a bungled attempt to cope with her broken home and bolster her self-esteem. A seemingly innocent decision to attend a concert proves to be a misstep which leads to another, and another, and yet another, ultimately catapulting her into a horrible dilemma with no apparent way out.

In desperation, Julie agrees to a scheme that Carmen, her lookalike, insists will be Julie's salvation. Their plan is risky, and Julie's resolve wavers, but Elvis's long-distance friendship and support give her strength. Renewed, she moves on, until fate intervenes in this "perfect plan" to turn back time and restore her innocence, leaving Julie alone in the heap of rubble that was once her life. How will she be able to escape the tragic consequences of her choices?

Can you ever hide from the truth?

Available in ebooks and paperback June 2017
ORDER NOW or LEARN MORE AT:
www.Pen-L.com/InThoseDazzlingDays.html

If you'd like to hear more about Josephine's upcoming books,
free deals, andother great Pen-L authors,
sign up for our Pals of Pen-L Newsletter here!
www.Pen-L.com/OptIn/Thanks.html

CLASSROOM DISCUSSION QUESTIONS FOR
In Those First Bright Days of Elvis

BEFORE READING THE BOOK:

1. Define "self-esteem." How does self-esteem influence your everyday life? Provide an example.

2. Do girls need a father figure in their lives? How about boys?

3. In the 1950s "Dilbert" was a label that defined kids who were not part of the popular crowd. Are there defining labels for those kids today? What are they?

4. How do you feel about kids in the popular groups? What about kids who are unpopular?

WHILE READING THE BOOK:

1. It is recommended that teachers play in the classroom some of the songs mentioned in the book, so that students can hear Elvis's work What is your impression of the 1950s? Would you have like to have been alive then? Why?

2. How are kids from the 1950s different from kids of today? What similarities are there? Give specific examples.

3. How are the parents of the 1950s different from parents of today? What similarities are there? Give specific examples.

4. Is there an in-crowd in your school? Are the kids who are a part of it nice? Cruel? Snobby?

AFTER READING THE BOOK:

5. In the book, Julie says she is fearful of her father and never wants to see him again. How does the absence of her father affect her life socially and emotionally?

6. What was your impression of Farrel? Do you think that Julie made the right choice concerning him?

7. A girl in the 1950s had limited choices regarding her future. Do you think things have changed for girls today, or are there still limitations? What are some?

8. Do you think the birth of rock 'n' roll brought major changes to everyday life, not just in the music world?

ADULT DISCUSSION QUESTIONS FOR
IN THOSE FIRST BRIGHT DAYS OF ELVIS

1. Did the birth of "rock 'n' roll" change the neighborhood/town in which you grew up? If so, how?

2. How were kids of the 1950s different from kids today? How are they similar?

3. How were parents of the 1950's different from parents of today? How are they similar?

4. What happens to the self-esteem of kids from broken homes?

5. How does the absence of a mother/father affect the lives of kids from broken homes?

6. Do girls need a father/mother figure in their lives? How about boys?

7. In the book, Julie says she is fearful of her father and never wants to see him again. How does the absence of her father affect her life socially and emotionally?

8. What were the choices of a girl who got pregnant out-of-wedlock in the 1950s?

9. What is Roe v. Wade? In the book, does the death from an illegal abortion make you want to see Roe v. Wade preserved as law or overthrown?

About the Author

Josephine Rascoe Keenan grew up in Arkansas's oil patch, El Dorado, city of "black gold." She began keeping a diary in the sixth grade, and classmates all the way through college still check in with her about "what happened when." After working many years in theatre as a director and professional actress doing plays, TV commercials, and featured roles in films, she undertook another creative venture, writing short stories, plays, and novels. *In Those First Bright Days of Elvis* takes readers back in time to an era when the world seemed brighter and more innocent, when folks had to stay home to get a phone call, when almost everybody loved Lucy, and when Rock 'n' Roll had just produced its first gyrations. It is remembered as a simpler time, but was it?

When not writing, Josephine enjoys oil painting, square dancing, and cooking Southern dishes—such as hot water cornbread, little lady peas, and grandma's peach cobbler—for her friends in Ohio where she lives with her husband and two feline princesses, Molly Underfoot and Katie Katherine Kalico.

Find Josephine At:

WWW.KeenanNovels.com

FJKeenan@fuse.net

Facebook Josephine.Keenan1

Twitter @FJKeenan1

Dear Readers,
If you enjoyed this book enough to review it for Goodreads, B&N, or Amazon.com, I'd appreciate it!
Thanks, Josephine

Find more great reads at
Pen-L.com

CPSIA information can be obtained
at www.ICGtesting.com
Printed in the USA
LVOW12s1505030817
543710LV00001B/111/P